DON'T THINK TWICE

You are so there.

T*WITCHES

T•WITCHES

**H.B. GILMOUR
& RANDI REISFELD**

SCHOLASTIC

NEW YORK   TORONTO   LONDON   AUCKLAND   SYDNEY
MEXICO CITY   NEW DELHI   HONG KONG   BUENOS AIRES

ISBN 0-439-24074-3

12 11 10 9 8 7 6 5 4 3 2 1   2 3 4 5 6 7/0

PRINTED IN THE U.S.A.   40
FIRST SCHOLASTIC PRINTING, JULY 2002

CHAPTER ONE
FRIDAY NIGHT

"Strike!"

Camryn Barnes yelped for joy and slapped palms with her bowling partner, Beth Fish. "We rock! We *are* the dream team!" Grinning triumphantly, Cam swiped a lock of chestnut hair off her face.

In the next lane, two cute guys from school — Jason, already crushed on Cam, and his blond-tipped friend Rick — checked her out. Cam returned their smiles. It felt excellent to be out with her buds, bowling, bragging, basking in the boy light.

"We *are* the alpha alley babes." Beth's freckled face was flushed with delight as she totaled up the score. To Kristen Hsu, their friend and, tonight, a member of the opposing team, she singsonged teasingly, "You'll never catch us!"

"Don't bet on it," came Kris's right-back-atcha response. With a toss of her gleaming black hair, she sent her own ball gliding down the alley. Perfect form, perfect release, perfect strike. "Deal," Kristen crowed. "We are so gonna pass you."

Good-naturedly, Cam pointed out, "One problem with your reasoning, Hsu-fly, the word 'we.' Your so-called teammate is AWOL."

Brianna Waxman, petite, blond, and one of their best friends, had wandered away again to take yet another call on her cell phone.

Brianna didn't seem right. It was as simple as that.

For one thing, Cam's most fashion-forward-trend friend had taken this giant leap backward — wearing economy-size sweatshirts that billowed nearly to her knees.

"Hey, Bree," Cam had teased a couple of weeks ago, "the eighties just called — they want their clothes back." Brianna had smiled weakly, but totally out of character, offered no sharp-tongued comeback.

Now Kristen called over loudly to Bree, "It's your turn. Come on! We can win this!"

Brianna didn't even turn around.

"Go fetch," Beth impishly instructed.

Kristen rolled her eyes and bounded up the steps toward the snack bar . . . where Bree, still cellularly involved, dismissed her with an impatient wave of her hand.

Kris paused, then Cam heard her say, "I'll go for you. I'm taking your turn, all right?"

In spite of her nagging feeling about Bree — and the bizarro stares Cam was getting from a pair of snaky-looking strangers, a tall boy and his squat brother, who thought she didn't notice them — Cam smiled. She was so up for tonight. It had nothing to do with bowling a strike, or even who won. She was having a Friday night out with her friends. Feeling good. Feeling normal.

It was the first time in weeks she'd felt that way.

Camped out on a bench one lane over, Camryn's sister, Alexandra Fielding, surveyed the scene and rolled her cool gray eyes. She was supposed to be bowling with Dylan, Cam's brother, except that she wasn't.

She'd been barred from playing. The bowling alley police had insisted she wear proper shoes — the kind they rented. Alex crossed her legs and smirked subversively. She loved her clunky, scuffed, dull brown combat boots. She wasn't taking them off.

She didn't want to be here.

And now that she'd been at this place, what was

it called — Toilet-Bowl-a-Rama? — for two excruciating hours, she hadn't changed her mind. She didn't want to be here even more.

But, of course, Cam did.

Make that: really, really did.

And why not? After nagging and ragging on Alex to come, there was her so-called twin — all snug low-rise jeans and too-cute T-shirt, color-coordinated down to her customized bowling shoes — playing princess of Bowl-a-Corn-Flakes. What a Britney!

Cam had tried to coax her into a similar outfit, but Alex had opted for a pair of Dylan's extreme skateboarding trous, wide in the waist, wider in the leg, hiked up to spotlight her scuffed Docs.

Eyeing her stubborn sister, Cam had declared, "Okay, it's a look, I'll give you that. Just top it with a crop that's circa now. Pick anything you want from my dresser."

So, of course, Alex had gone into her own dresser and pulled out a mud-brown turtleneck. Ditto for accessories.

"Well, at least use my old bowling shoes. You don't want to rent a pair," Cam urged. "I mean, yuck, who knows who used them last? And we can share my custom bowling ball."

"So not," was Alex's answer.

"But you'll bowl better with it. Our fingers are exactly the same size."

Same clothing size, same shoe size, same-size fingers.

Same extraordinary charcoal-rimmed gray eyes, blunt-tipped noses, full lips.

What would have been the same exact thick, wavy auburn hair, except that Alex was constantly changing hers. This morning, she'd dyed her formerly platinum-bleached spikes an extremely hot fire-engine red.

If attitudes came in sizes, those of Camryn Barnes and Alexandra Fielding would be at opposite ends of the rack.

Day and night. Sugar and spice. They were as far apart as the shimmering ocean that bordered Cam's native Massachusetts and the craggy peaks that soared above Alex's Montana home.

Separated at birth, they'd grown up apart for fourteen of their fifteen years. They'd not even known of each other's existence until — Alex calculated — could it really be only ten months ago that they'd met?

And discovered that they were not just twins, but witches. T'Witches — with strange and powerful abilities to do things, see and hear things, that others could not.

For instance, Alex could listen in on thoughts. A fun talent sometimes, embarrassing at others. And occasionally totally irritating — like tonight. Like right now, hearing the strange bowling brothers discussing her and Cam from behind the lanes. *Think they're so special, just 'cause they're twins,* the thickset one was sneering. Giving off nasty stalker vibes, his tall bro was thinking, *So they're the ones.*

Yeech. Alex's stomach heaved, as if she'd swallowed sour milk. She looked over at her sister. And caught Cam glancing at her disapprovingly and thinking, *Oh, come on, Als. Let yourself go for one night. Let's just have* fun.

Let it go? Let the most important thing that had happened since they'd discovered each other go? Take a reality break for a night out bowling? Pretend that they weren't different from other kids and hadn't just discovered that the mother they'd never met might actually be alive?! Cam's timing reeked.

A fact Alex had pointed out to her earlier, in no uncertain terms.

A fact that Camryn had totally twisted, trying to guilt Alex into agreeing.

"After all we've been through, we deserve a fun night out with my — I mean, our — friends," Cam had insisted.

Alex knew exactly what she meant. But chose to zone in on only one part of her sister's sentence. "Right the first time, dude: *your* friends."

Now, bored at the bowling alley, she couldn't decide which one of Cam's best buds annoyed her more.

Beth, tall, freckled, and kinky-haired, who Alex usually liked, was all her sister's slavish shadow tonight, the wind beneath Cam-I-Am's wings.

Then there was Kristen, hypercompetitive and deeply devoted to all things Brianna, no matter that Bree was being incredibly rude to her right now. As usual, Kris had the diminutive trendoid's back and was covering for her.

And least but not last, Brianna Waxman, the plastic, sarcastic guru of gossip, who'd recently, mysteriously traded in her skintight designer duds for generic XXL cover-ups. In Alex's not-so-humble opinion, superficial and snotty nailed Bree.

"They're your friends, too, if you'd let them be," Cam had whined. "Give me a break. For one night I want to be . . . just . . . regular again — "

"Regular, rich, and popular?"

"You know what I mean," Cam insisted. "Average, ordinary, usual, normal. Come on, Als, let's just have fun."

Fun?

All at once, a mischievous smile played across Alex's lips. Okay, she responded silently to her sister's plea, let's have fun.

CHAPTER TWO
A DISTRESS SIGNAL

Kristen had come back to her lane and was about to take Brianna's turn. She stopped suddenly, narrowing her piercing black eyes at Alex.

Hmmm . . . the evil twin, Alex heard Kris muse. *Miss Iodine Head. What makes me think she can really help?*

Case in point again, Alex told herself. Reading random minds really was sometimes more a pain than a present. Did she really want to know what was on Kristen's so-called mind?

What makes me think she can help? Where was Kristen-the-cutthroat going with that? Did she think she could get Alex to change her shoes and play for Bree?

Whatever her plan, Kristen canceled it abruptly and returned to the game. As she'd done before, she released her personal pink-and-gray bowling ball expertly and sent it rumbling down the center of the lacquered wooden lane.

Evil twin? Iodine Head?

Maybe I *can* get in this game, Alex thought, her lips twisting into a playful smile. She glanced at the one person in the room who could read *her* mind and stop her from what she was about to do. But Cam was flirting outrageously with Jason and his friend Captain Peroxide. Not paying any attention to her. Which left the coast clear for . . .

Alex called up a "fun" image in her mind, then focused on Kristen's ball, which was halfway down the lane.

Exactly as she'd pictured it, the pink-and-gray globe stopped dead — and, as if someone had put an awesome spin on it, reversed its direction. Gathering speed, it rolled backward, aiming straight at Kris!

Kristen's jaw dropped as she scrambled out of the way. "What the . . ."

"That's how you take my turn for me?" Brianna, the sweatshirt-draped diva, scolded as she bounced over to the lane. "At least when I bowl, the ball doesn't boomerang!"

"I didn't do that!" Kristen, aghast, managed to sputter, bending down to catch and examine the wayward ball. "I don't know how that happened."

Cam's attention was finally caught by the commotion. *All I asked for was one night off, one normal night of bowling with my buds,* she grumbled telepathically at her twin, who was staring innocently at the ceiling. *Too much to ask? I don't think so.*

"Let's see," Beth teased, pretending to write on the score sheet. "By my calculations, that counts for a minus ten."

"Do over!" Kris pronounced, hands on her hips. "Anyway, now that Bree's here, she can bowl for herself."

Bree went to pick up the ball. For a moment, her hand shook. As if the ball were too heavy for her.

Just then, her phone rang again. She checked the caller ID. "Gotta take this one. It's my dad again, so it's about the party."

The party. Right. Another scene Alex was eager to skip. Another fun fete Cam was trying to guilt her into.

Brianna's dad, long divorced from her mom, lived in California, where he was a hotshot movie producer. The main thing he produced for Bree was disappointment. He was constantly making and breaking promises to her. Even this "birthday" party was to make up for one he'd bailed out on the week Bree actually turned fifteen.

Alex got up, stretched, and mindlessly glanced over at the snack bar where Bree was taking her father's call. At first, all Alex heard were balls rumbling, pins falling, kids screaming, bad music blaring. Then, above the bowling alley din, a conversation.

"I'm sorry, Miss Waxman," a clipped male voice said. "He didn't say why."

Alex's forehead furrowed as she wondered who was speaking. Suddenly, her gray eyes widened. It was Brianna's phone convo she'd tuned in to! By accident. Haphazardly. Totally by chance.

Or was it?

She definitely hadn't tried to listen in. Anything Brianna Waxman had to say was of less than zero interest. Plus, even with the hyperhearing that was one of Alex's witchy "gifts," she might have been able to catch Bree's half of the call, but not what some snotty guy on the other end of the phone had to say.

Did that mean her picking up on it wasn't entirely random?

Working their gifts was still kind of new to her and Cam.

They'd learned that their strange talents — Alex's superhearing and her recently demonstrated ability to move things — like bowling balls — just by thinking about them; and Cam's premonitions, visions, ability to see things at great distances in microscopic detail — became especially strong when they were needed to help someone out of a jam.

Which was not what was happening here. Was it?

"Again?" Bree's voice sounded way more helpless than Alex had ever heard it before. "Why can't he come to the phone this time? We have to make plans. It's tomorrow night — I've already invited everyone."

The merciless response on the other end was all business, making no attempt to hide a lack of interest. "Your father said he'd call you later. There's really nothing more I can say or do. It is three hours earlier here and he is still working."

It was, Alex realized, Bree's fickle father's personal assistant on the phone from California.

No, no, not again, please not this time, Alex heard Bree's inner plea. *He promised.*

"He'll call you later," the assistant repeated.

"What time?" Bree asked.

"He didn't tell me. I'm sorry." The jerk didn't sound the least bit sorry, Alex thought.

He doesn't care about me, even on my birthday. What's wrong with me? Why doesn't he love me? It's because I'm fat, ugly, stupid . . . If she hadn't heard Bree's despair, Alex would have laughed.

Brianna Waxman, the flawless makeup artist, blond-on-blond girl, thin as a dime, actually thought she was ugly? Wake up and smell the mirror. But Bree, who could shrivel a loudmouth with a look, said pathetically, "Well, do you know if he's flying to Marble Bay tonight? For my birthday party?"

"Miss Waxman, really, I wouldn't know anything about that."

Alex felt a stab of pain for Bree. Was her dad really going to blow off the party that was to make up for the party he'd canceled last time?

Brianna came back to the alley, a smile pasted on her wan face. Loud enough for everyone to hear, she announced, "That was my dad. Again! This is like the fifth time he's called tonight. This party is going to rock!"

Alex looked down at her skuzzy combat boots, afraid to catch Bree's eye. Did Cam, she wondered, have a clue about what was going on?

"Excellent," Kris said. "Come over, Jason and Rick are joining us —" Cam, Beth, and Kris, too, it seemed, had given up bowling for boyage. Alex looked up and saw that they were all in one lane now, with the high-school hotties who'd been flirting with Cam.

With that bogus smile masking her disappointment, Brianna headed their way . . . until a gel-haired guy in a bicep-baring shirt and skintight jeans came up behind her and tapped her shoulder.

Alex knew who he was: Marco Paulsen, Bree's crush. He was in the drama club at Marble Bay High, their star actor. Cam and company suspected that he was only into Bree because of her dad's Hollywood connections. Privately, they called him Marco Polo, an adventurer exploring ways to use people. But Marco was dimpled and ripped, an eye candy arm-piece, and Bree's date for the party.

Well, maybe something'll go right for her tonight, Alex found herself hoping.

Bree whirled around and lit up. "Marco!" she purred. "Just the guy I was looking for."

Marco cocked his head. "You were?"

"Of course." Bree smiled. "I want to tell you about tomorrow night."

"Uh, yeah, about that . . ." Marco said, sheepishly looking away — toward a redhead a few feet from them. "I can't make it."

"You're kidding." When Bree saw he wasn't, she fought to keep her voice light. "Why not?"

Marco sighed dramatically. "Something's come up."

Over Marco's shoulder, Bree saw the tall redhead eyeing him. "That girl over there? Is that what came up?" she blurted.

Marco grinned, shrugged. "She's got tickets to the Bruins game. What can I say?"

"But I was . . . it's going to be, like . . . the best party." Bree's eyes were filling with tears.

Marco put on his Mr. Sensitivity face and chucked Bree under the chin as if she were a dog. "Hey, hey, don't take it so hard," he said, using his soap opera voice. "What can I do? It's the biggest game of the year."

"Sure," Bree managed to whisper. Inside, she was frantic. *What am I going to say? What am I going to tell everyone? This is so awful, so . . . humiliating.*

Alex was ballistic.

She wished Bree could read *her* mind: *Say he couldn't come, 'cause he accidentally died — of humiliation!*

Inspiration rocked her! Alex gazed at Marco's oh-so-cool undone high-tops and pictured the funniest thing happening. What if, while he was busy brushing Brianna off, his shoelaces started squirming? And while he was breaking Bree's already fragile heart, the laces from his left shoe got tangled up with the long laces of his right? Got sort of twisted into a knot — like the knot he was making in Bree's gut — so that as soon as he started to walk away . . .

"Aarrghh!" Marco screamed as he went down. Hard.

Alex had totally counted on his pants splitting — which they did with a gratifying rip. She hadn't counted on them exposing the dorkiest Captain America under-

pants anyone had ever seen. The whole bowling alley —
gawking and laughing at him. That was a very cool surprise.

And when Marco tried to get up, only to slip on his
butt again and crack his coccyx?

An unexpected bonus.

CHAPTER THREE
THE FIRST NOTE

"Poor Marco," Alex gloated, when they got home and closed the door to their shared bedroom. "With his caboose out of commission, he won't be able to sit through a drama class, let alone a Bruins game. You should be thanking me."

Cam had many things on her mind. Thanking Alex was not one of them. "He really got hurt! How many times have Karsh and Ileana told us: We don't use our powers to injure the innocent."

It was true. Ileana, their headstrong guardian witch, had reminded them of this several times. And, of course, so had Karsh, the wise old warlock who was Ileana's guardian. Both were charged with teaching the twins

how to use their strange and, at times, unpredictable powers properly.

"Even if the innocent is a raging rat hurting someone you care about?" Alex asked. "If you chill for five seconds, I'll tell you what happened."

When she finished recounting Brianna's bummer,
from birthday desertion to date despair, Alex assumed
Cam would apologize or at least lighten up.

Wrong. Her sister was still in a funk. "You can't just
go poking into other people's brains whenever you feel
like it," Cam grumbled, beginning to undress.

"Hello, don't you get it? I didn't *choose* to overhear
Bree's long-distance call, it just happened."

"Whatever," Cam said dismissively.

"You know what?" Alex was so over her sister's bad
mood. "I've got more important things to think about."
And so do you! she thought.

Cam picked up on the unspoken remark right away.
"Oh, give it a rest," she muttered.

"Whoops, my bad," Alex said sarcastically, plopping
down on her bed and pulling off her boots. "I mean, having a nice, normal night out is way more urgent than —"

"I care!" Cam snapped. "I want to find our mother as
much as you do! I just . . . There are other things to con-
sider. Everything's not as simple as you'd like it to be."

Alex didn't need eyes as sharp as Cam's to see that

her twin was wrestling with an issue: an issue named Emily Barnes.

Emily and David Barnes were the couple who had adopted Cam as an infant. Unlike Sara Fielding, who'd been Alex's adoptive mom, Emily was alive and well.

And so, it now seemed, was Miranda, the twin's biological mother.

Well, alive anyway.

Last summer, right after Sara's death, Alex had felt the same way Cam did now, she guessed. She'd had no interest in finding the stranger who'd given birth to them and then vanished. Back then, Sara Fielding was the only mom Alex had ever known — or wanted to know.

But recently she and Cam had stumbled onto evidence that Miranda might be hidden away in an institution, receiving visits from the twins' brutal uncle Thantos.

Lord Thantos, a burly, black-bearded tracker, was the beast who'd murdered their father, Aron.

It was Karsh and Ileana who had found Aron dead. And it was Ileana who had sheltered the newborn twins in her arms as their mother's sorrow and shock gave way to madness.

Wild with grief, Miranda had vanished that very night. Whether she'd wandered into the harsh wilderness of Coventry or thrown herself into the icy waters surrounding the island, no one knew for sure. But she had not been seen or heard from in fifteen years. She was assumed dead.

Since then, Ileana was convinced, Thantos had been trying to lure, catch, and kill Aron and Miranda's children. Thantos and a third brother, Fredo, had been in pursuit of the twins for years. But thank goodness Fredo was as weak and ridiculous as his older brother, Thantos, was strong and terrifying.

"I'm taking a shower," Cam informed her sister, and closed the door to the bathroom that separated their room from Dylan's.

"Good," Alex responded, peeling off her socks. "Make it a cold one. You need to chill."

"Right," Cam barked back. "And you need to stop obsessing!"

Like that was possible, Alex thought as she heard the shower water revving full force. She reached over and pulled the trashy newspaper *Starstruck* out of Cam's bowling bag. It was the kind of supermarket rag that headlined stories about alien invasions, dead celebrity sightings, and the birth of three-headed monster sharks. There, on the cover of last week's edition, was Uncle Thantos.

BILLIONAIRE RECLUSE SNAPPED BY STARSTRUCK'S INTREPID

CAMERAMAN was plastered across the front page under the hulking warlock's furious face. And then, SEE PG. 4.

Alex didn't have to turn to page four. She'd practically memorized the article. It was captioned *Camera-shy technology billionaire, Lord Thantos DuBaer, enters celebrity clinic,* and it speculated on what illness the computer tycoon was seeking help for.

Alex stared again at the picture of their sneering uncle, then tried to decipher the fuzzy black-and-white images behind him. Could she and Cam have missed something as they'd pored over that photograph? No, there was still no nameplate on the institution's door, no reference in the story to the name or location of the celebrity clinic. There was, however, a spiny shrub that looked like a palm tree.

Cam had zoned in on the plant days ago and had sarcastically pointed out that it narrowed their search to Florida, Hawaii, and every warm-weather site in between.

But if they could find the "intrepid" cameraman who'd taken the picture, they could find the sanitarium.

And they had to find it. To find her.

The rag-mag *Starstruck* had gotten it wrong. Thantos wasn't a patient. He was a visitor, and the patient he'd been to see was Miranda. Their mother. They had no hard evidence, just Cam's premonition and Alex's belief in it.

Cam *had* e-mailed *Starstruck* right away. She'd left her cell phone number on multiple voice mails but so far no one had gotten back to her. Tonight, she didn't even seem to care.

Cam had been first to push, Alex recalled, pulling her wrinkled turtleneck over her head, to jump on the we've-got-to-find-our-real-mom express.

And now she was backing down. Why would she insist on a stupid night of bowling, a major delay tactic, when they should have been spending every minute trying to find Miranda?

And what if we do find her? Cam was thinking at that exact moment. *What happens to us, to my family, to Mom, especially? What's going to happen to Emily?*

I knew it! Alex barged in telepathically. *You're more worried about hurting Emily's feelings than finding our real mother.*

I may be in the shower, Alex, but you're the one who's all wet, Cam shot back, shutting off the water. Stepping out onto the bath mat, she wrapped herself in a towel, a big, thick, still-fluffy-from-the-dryer towel that felt warm, clean, and safe — like her life, like bowling with her buds, like home. . . .

"Busted!" Alex flung open the bathroom door and pointed an accusing finger at her startled sister. "You're wimping on me. Now that we're close to finding her, you're backpedaling. What are you really afraid of?"

"You!" Cam shot back. "You and your prying, brain-busting, thought-lifting ESP ears. Not even the shower is a sanctuary from your snooping! Besides, you obviously know what I was thinking —"

"Let me guess. You were cherishing your oh-so-boring existence?" In spite of her irritation, Alex handed Cam another towel to wrap around her dripping hair. "You are scared that finding Miranda will shatter your sheltered life for good? Or could it be your perfect parents you're worried about? Afraid that making contact with our birth mom will drive Emily around the bend?"

Cam bit her lip and turned away. Hugging the towel around her, she said into the steamy mirror, "Things will be different, Als, when we find Miranda. There's no way they can't be."

"We don't know what we'll find, or if we'll even find her," Alex pointed out. "So it's a little soon to freak. You're suffering from premature wig-out."

Cam touched Alex's elbow. "We will find her. You and me together, we can do pretty much anything we set our minds and witchy talents to. Even if we are just —"

Unconsciously, she rubbed her gold sun pendant between her thumb and forefinger. The charm hung on a chain around her neck. Cam rarely took it off.

"Fledglings," Alex finished the sentence. "That's what Karsh calls us."

"Right," Cam agreed. "Beginners. But one day we'll be what he and Ileana are. Top-ranked witches. Trackers. And that means we'll be able to track her, to find her."

"One day," Alex repeated, frustrated. "One day it'll be too late." Instinctively, her fingers sought the gold half-moon charm hanging from her necklace.

Their birth father, Aron, had made them the amulets. He'd made only one other: a linked sun and moon charm for his wife, their lost mother, Miranda.

Cam shooed her sister out of the bathroom and managed a weak smile. Her life had taken a shocking twist when Alexandra Fielding, dragging a scrungy little duffel bag and a weighty chip on her shoulder, had come into it.

But no one in the world knew her like Alex did. Growing up, Cam had *done* all the normal things, but — like the dazzling sun without its shadow-casting counterpart, the moon — she'd never felt whole. Before Alex, she wasn't.

"What's that paper?" she asked minutes later, coming into their bedroom, buttoning her soft flannel pj's.

Alex was on the bed in one of Sara's worn T-shirts. "Oh, it's just the one with Thantos's picture on the cover."

"No, not that." Cam pointed. "The piece of paper on the floor near my bowling bag."

Alex shrugged. "Must've fallen out when I snagged the copy of *Starstruck*."

Cam scooped up the folded sheet, opened it, and gasped. Typed in wildly different fonts was an unsigned message: She needs you. **Only you** can save her.

CHAPTER FOUR
FREDO'S TRIAL

The Coventry Island Unity Council was in session. Lady Rhianna, the Exalted Elder in charge, sat in her plush chair at the center of the amphitheater. Lord Grivveniss and Lady Fan flanked Rhianna.

A trial was about to begin. The entire community, it seemed, was abuzz and in attendance. A member of the exalted DuBaer family, long suspected of misuse of magick, now stood accused of a more serious crime. Fredo, the clan's youngest and most inept DuBaer, had caused havoc since childhood. In a moment, Lady Rhianna would read the charges lodged against him. Then, an advocate would present the People's case, followed by a supporter for the Accused, who would defend the wayward warlock.

The verdict would eventually be rendered by a group of Coventry Island Elders, who occupied the first three rows of the amphitheater.

Lord Karsh fit neatly into that category, but he was not sitting among his peers. The aged warlock had achieved Exalted Elder status long ago and was one of the most revered members of the Coventry community.

Today, he and Ileana, the imperious young witch he'd reared, would play a different role. They were to be the voice of the People. Karsh had been chosen to present the case and paid rapt attention as the plump, wiry-haired Rhianna cleared her throat, about to begin.

"Fredo DuBaer," she called, her deep voice echoing through the packed chamber, "has been accused of numerous misdeeds, including unauthorized shape-shifting, using his magick to terrorize rather than heal, and — the most serious offense —"

Ileana should have been keenly attentive, but lost in thought, she barely heard the charges.

Her guardian, Karsh, his craggy white face wearing the friendly grin that so often frightened fledglings, elbowed her gently. "They'll be safe," he whispered to the preoccupied young witch.

"Ha!" Ileana exclaimed too loudly. "Safe is so not their style."

They were speaking of Camryn and Alexandra, born Artemis and Apolla on Coventry Island. Born, Ileana reminded herself with a shudder, into a family whose name called up as much fear, awe, and envy as it did admiration. The DuBaer dynasty had produced generations of great witches and warlocks. And in those generations, most had used their power and wealth for good — but there were others who had opted for evil.

Lady Rhianna was reciting the major charge levied against Fredo. ". . . breaking the terms of his parole by leaving the island without notifying the Council and attempting to forcibly abduct innocent fledglings —"

"The twin daughters of Aron and Miranda?" Lady Fan interrupted, smiling slyly. "They are young but not exactly innocent. I hear they're quite clever for unschooled witches. And they are the Accused's family."

Sensing danger, Ileana looked up at last. "Does that make his kidnapping attempts any less monstrous?" she demanded.

"Well, it is a point worth considering," the dotty Lord Grivveniss announced, nodding as solemnly as a dashboard dog. "It might be considered a mitigating circumstance, eh? Perhaps Fredo was merely trying to introduce himself to his nieces. After all, he'd never met them. Perhaps that's why he left the island without permission, eh? Compelled by love of family —"

"Love of family!" Ileana leaped to her feet.

"Exalted Elders." Karsh stepped in front of her. "If Fredo had wanted to see his nieces he could have done so many years ago, when their proud father invited both his brothers — Thantos as well as Fredo — to enter his home and meet them. Instead, Aron was lured outside and murdered —"

"Yes, murdered by his own brother," Ileana hollered from behind her guardian.

"Enough!" Lady Rhianna cut her off. Rising from her thronelike chair she began pacing before the bench where Karsh and Ileana stood. "Your accusation has never been proved, Ileana. I challenged you to bring Lord Thantos before this Council to present his side of the story and you failed at that —"

"I failed?" Ileana laughed bitterly. "All Coventry has failed. Thantos sends computers and gifts and money to the Council and the hunt for him is sidelined. He is wanted for questioning in the death of my charges' father, but his gifts are accepted and no one —"

"You insult the Council!" Indignant, Lady Fan drew herself up but, as she was barely four and a half feet tall, the gesture seemed more comical than commanding.

"Still, we are grateful, young witch," Rhianna said,

stepping between Fan and Ileana, "that you returned Fredo DuBaer to Coventry. He is a nuisance and, some think, a disgrace to our kind. Yet he deserves to be heard."

During Fredo's arraignment a week earlier, it had been decided that Karsh would speak on behalf of the community. The problem had been finding an advocate for Fredo.

"Impossible," Lady Fan had despaired as the trio of Exalted Elders had discussed it. "Who on this island would stand up for that troubled creature? I doubt that there's a respectable witch or warlock who would take his case."

Before Fan completed her sentence, the amphitheater was rocked by a sudden quake. The sunlight that had poured through the building's glass dome turned cloudy. Darkness descended on the Council chamber.

"He's here," Ileana had whispered, trembling.

Karsh had nodded silently and allowed her to curl, childlike, into his arms.

A darkness within the darkness stirred. A purple light spilled from the lining of a large black cape, casting a violet glow over the chamber and outlining a tall, bearded figure. A deep, angry voice bellowed, "I will stand up for my brother."

The cloud that had shadowed the dome blew past, allowing daylight back into the room.

"Lord Thantos." Lady Rhianna smiled at the hulking, black-bearded tracker. "It's been a long time since we've had the pleasure of your company on Coventry Island."

A scornful smile curled Thantos's lips. He bowed mockingly. "Pleasure? We'll soon see if it's pleasure that I bring. Lords and Ladies, Exalted Elders," he said, ignoring Ileana, "let the trial begin!"

CHAPTER FIVE
A CHANGE IN PLANS

The note that had fallen out of Cam's bowling bag was about Miranda. That was what they'd finally decided. *She needs you. Only you can save her.*

Someone, Thantos or one of his spies, was Alex's guess, had realized that they were on Miranda's trail.

But what if it was Karsh or Ileana, Cam wondered, telling them their mother was in trouble?

Had the strangely typed message been sent by friend or foe?

Wrestling with the answer had given Cam and Alex a fitful night's sleep. Without planning to, they'd risen before anyone else in the household and continued where they'd left off.

"It's got to be from Karsh," Cam declared as the twins padded quietly down to the kitchen.

Cam opened the towering two-door fridge and pulled out a box of strawberries and a container of skim milk."

"I don't buy it," Alex countered, raking a hand through her crimson hair.

From the freezer Cam scooped out a handful of ice cubes. *What don't you buy? Besides decent clothes and a hairstylist . . .*

"1 heard that," Alex warned, nudging Cam aside so she could get a box of Pop-Tarts. "Dude, when has Karsh ever contacted us by some cheesy computer note? I doubt if he even owns a PC. Not his way, never was. Plus, he doesn't actually know what happened to Miranda, does he?"

"Guess not," Cam said, tossing berries, milk, a banana, and ice cubes into the blender. She added a packet of vitamin C. "You want?" she offered Alex. "I should have enough here for both of us."

Alex squashed her first response, which was "I'd rather drink paint," and managed a polite "I'll pass."

"So if our mystery author isn't Karsh, then who?" Cam asked, dropping a capsule of echinacea into her brew.

"Well, it sure isn't Ileana's style." Alex jammed a

Pop-Tart into the toaster. "Our reluctant guardian either uses e-mail or makes a dramatic appearance."

Cam laughed. If Ileana had wanted to tell them something or warn them of some danger or help them — she'd have swept into their room, nose in the air, midnight-blue cape flaring around her Jimmy Choo stilettos. Stuffing a note into her bowling case? Ne-vuh!

That left . . .

"Thantos," Alex said.

"Final answer?" Cam dismissed the notion. "How unlikely is it that a billionaire recluse, as *Starstruck* called our uncle, would deign to show up at Bowl-a-Trauma? He'd send a messenger. . . ."

"And the nominees are?" Alex asked.

"You do realize you're about to ingest pure sugar, guaranteed to rot your teeth, eat away your stomach, and for the bonus round, fill you with empty calories." Cam frowned as her sister pulled the Pop-Tart from the toaster.

"Breakfast of champions," Alex retorted, deliberately biting off a big piece.

"What about those two sketchy-looking skanks who were checking us out?"

Cam arched her eyebrows. "You noticed them, too?"

"Who wouldn't? They stood out like festering sores. Could be one of them was the messenger."

"Messenger? In the bowling alley? Was one of you expecting a package?" Dylan Barnes sauntered into the kitchen, rubbed his eyes, and yawned.

Cam and Alex looked at him, then exchanged wary glances. *Dylan?* Cam silently asked her sister.

Thantos and his followers were talented shape-shifters. Masquerading as someone Cam and Alex knew and trusted was not beyond them.

"No way," Alex decided.

"And, backspace," Dylan added. "What are you two doing up? Did the rooster forget to tell you it's Saturday?"

"Right back atcha," Cam queried.

"I'm going boarding with Robbie Meeks." Dylan grabbed the box of Pop-Tarts Alex had left out. "We're getting an early start." In one smooth motion, he shoved two half-thawed Pop-Tarts into the crumb-ringed toaster and grabbed milk from the fridge, downing it in a few gulps.

"Who's taking you to Robbie's?" Alex asked.

"Mom or Dad, whoever gets up first," Dylan responded.

"Mom," Cam said absentmindedly, forgetting for a moment that Dylan didn't know about her hypersenses. "She's up already."

"And she hears a phone ringing," Alex added.

"How do you know?" Dylan started to ask.

A split second later, Emily called from upstairs, "Cam, your cell phone is ringing. You want me to get it?"

Dylan's milky mouth dropped open.

"Coincidence!" Alex tried to assure him.

"I'm on it!" Cam hollered to her mom, heading for the stairs.

Alex raced into their room behind Cam and closed the door. "*Starstruck* calling back?" she asked hopefully.

"Finally," Cam said.

"I was just about to leave a message." The voice on the other end of the line was hyper upbeat, with a nervous edge.

Alex sank down on her bed. It wasn't *Starstruck*'s photo editor returning Cam's call, it was Cam's starstruck friend, Brianna Waxman. No doubt the call was about her party. Though Alex still didn't want to go, she found herself hoping it was on, hoping Bree's old man hadn't bailed again.

"How sweet is this?" Alex heard Brianna chirping. "My dad can't come here, so he's flying me there. We're leaving for L.A. in an hour — first-class tickets are at the airport. We'll be there through Monday, back at school Tuesday."

"That's . . . great . . . I guess," Cam stammered.

"I know you're bummed, everyone is," Brianna said. "It's so totally last minute. But my dad's staff is working overtime to throw a Hollywood mega-bash in my honor."

"So you're uninviting us? I mean, we're not coming with you. Obviously." Cam glanced at Alex, knowing her twin was tuning in.

"Sorry," Bree said. "Daddy only sprang for two tickets. I asked Kristen. You understand, right?"

"No probs." Alex plucked the phone out of Cam's hand and told Bree, "We're totally down with it."

"No, we're not!" Cam contradicted, taking back the phone. She barely knew why she'd said it. "I mean, do you think this is a good idea, Bree?"

"It's the *kick* idea!" Bree shot back. "Daddy, mansion, Brad, Julia, Brice, a spread in *People* magazine. The downside would be?"

Cam bit her lip. What should she say? Her friend sounded psyched, excited. Her deadbeat dad was finally coming through for her. After what Alex had told her about last night, Cam should have been thrilled and relieved for Bree. Still, she couldn't stop herself from saying, "It's just that you've been, I don't know, tired or something lately. Do you really think jetting off cross-country, just for the weekend . . . I know it's your birthday, but it'll take a lot out of you." How lame did that sound?

The only thing that'll make it lamer is if you re-mind her to wear her retainer and clean up her room, Alex shot at Cam.

"A few days of Cali sunshine does a body good. It is still winter here, in case you hadn't noticed," Bree said.

Cam couldn't argue with that. Her bedroom window framed a gray tableau — gray sky, bare gray trees, gray-streaked mush from the last snowfall. And a fresh layer of the powdery stuff was forecast over the weekend.

Plus, Bree's emotional meter was set on gush. "My dad just got this new gym installed. State-of-the-art exercise equipment!"

Brianna had become such the gym bunny lately. But how could Cam stress over healthy exercise?

"Favor?" Bree said. "My mom is going to call the school and say I'm out sick, so cover for me, okay? Don't go blabbing about my phenomenal West Coast birthday bender."

"Sure," Alex agreed as Cam stared into space, not an-swering her burbling bud.

"Okay, well, I've got a bunch of calls to make before the limo comes. Tootles, twinskis," Brianna shrilled, then hung up.

Cam hit END and put her phone down. "Als, some-thing's not right with Bree."

Alex agreed, "All the more reason she needs this ego-booster shot."

"Sure, if her dad doesn't . . ." Cam didn't finish. She didn't have to. Alex knew what she was thinking.

"Let's be optimistic." Alex channeled Oprah and hoped she was better at convincing Cam than she was at convincing herself. "Miracles do happen, you know."

"Speaking of . . ." Alex reminded her.

"Right. We'll give *Starstruck* until the end of the day Monday," Cam decided. "If they don't call by then, we'll . . ."

"Find another way to get to them," Alex finished her sentence. "And track down the photographer who took that picture. No matter who sent the note — good guy trying to help or bad guy trying to trick us — we have to find her. Fast. That picture is our only lead."

CHAPTER SIX
A VISION IN THE SNOW

Alex had been a sophomore at Cam's school, Marble Bay High, since September, a grand total of eight months. Unlike her old school, Crow Creek Regional, with its peeling, puke-green walls and ancient computers, Marble Bay was all fresh all the time.

Translation: better 'hood, better stuff.

The school was best of breed. Spankin' new everything: computer lab, library, media room. More electives to choose from, more clubs to join, more guidance counselors to whine to.

More didn't necessarily mean better. And yet, Alex admitted as she headed toward her locker between classes on Monday, the school did get Alex's props for its art department, especially the elective called Art-ventures. Student creations from that class — all on the theme of friendship — decorated the corridor she was walking down now.

One project in particular caught Alex's eye: a collage. She was sure she'd never seen it before, though something about it seemed familiar. It showed two girls — definitely not twins. One was very thin. You could see her skeleton, make out the bones inside her transparent body. Only her eyes were impenetrable. The other was so fat she appeared to be exploding; bits of the paper that made up her form were actually torn in places. The picture was dotted with cutouts of food, and there were letters pasted over the fat girl's mouth, letters of different sizes and styles that spelled out the word *Secrets.* It almost looked as if she were choking on them.

Cool. Alex didn't totally get it, but whoever had thought it up had some weird but interesting ideas about friendship. Alex nearly took her props back when she saw who'd signed it: Kristen Hsu.

"Can you believe Kristen did that?" someone behind her asked.

Alex jumped involuntarily, then recognized Sukari's voice and turned, grinning, to greet the girl. Of Cam's Six Pack of best buds, Sukari Woodward was the one Alex liked best. Cocoa-skinned, like Alex's Montana homey

Evan, Sukari had round glasses, a round face, and a defiantly round bod. Her platinum-bleached dreads and Gap/
Banana clothes, however, were state-of-the-mall, befitting
the daughter of two distinguished doctors.

"Ready for the test?" Sukari asked as they headed
toward chemistry class. "I spent half the weekend studying for it."

Reality bite: Suke was a super science-head. If it had
taken her all weekend to study, Alex was in trouble. She
and Cam had been stressed and obsessed since receiving
the anonymous note. Little else had penetrated her brain.
In the "else" category is where the chemistry test lay, un-
attended to.

The "uh-oh" look on her face gave her away. "Spaced
on it?" Sukari guessed.

"Totally," Alex conceded as they approached their
row of lockers. "There was a lot of other stuff going on."

Sukari pursed her lips. "Can't blame it on Brianna's
party. Bet you're relieved to get out of that one."

Alex tossed her books into her locker. "Was I that
obvious?"

"Is L'il Kim?" Sukari slipped a notebook into her
backpack. "Some things, girl, are written all over you."

Ten minutes later, Alex found herself wishing the
notes to the science test were written all over her. The questions might as well have been in Elvish. She could barely de-

cipher them, forget about figuring out the right answers. She scanned the classroom and saw some kids chewing on pencils or staring into space, looking worried. Others, Sukari among them, were scribbling away confidently.

A random thought drifted into Alex's head. Would it really be cheating if she lightly knocked on someone's — say, Sukari's — brain, just to see what she was thinking?

Bam! Like a speeding billiard ball crashing into that idle thought, came another, effectively knocking the first idea out of her head. *What are you thinking? You'd use your powers to cheat on a test?*

Alex almost laughed out loud and sent a zinger back to Camryn the chem cop. *I'm using my powers like we're supposed to. To help the needy — which in this case is me!* Before Cam could slam her with another telepathic tsk-tsk, Alex added, *Chill. I am about to fail this test all on my own. No amount of magick could give CPR to my grade in this class.*

The final thought Cam imparted was: *The word on Mrs. Olsen: On multiple choice, it's usually "C, B, D, A."*

As Alex circled her first *C,* she realized this was the first time Cam had contacted her from as far away as another classroom. Now that was new.

"What's it like on your planet?" Beth tapped Cam on the shoulder, startling her. "I said hi, *hola, shalom, bon-*

jour. . . . Wherever you are, I'm obviously out of the language loop."

Cam looked at Beth blankly. She hadn't even realized her best friend had slid into the seat across the aisle.

"My bad," Cam apologized. "But I'm totally here now."

"People! People! Settle down. We have a lot to cover," their language arts teacher, with the unfortunate name of Mr. Snibble, called out. At least he had a sense of humor. "Don't quibble with Snibble" was the motto on his blackboard.

Holding a stack of papers, he said, "Since, as you're about to see, you all performed so brilliantly — yes, I am kidding — I'm giving you the chance to redeem yourselves and your sagging grades."

Cam was bummed. Her GPA was crucial, and obviously Snibble hadn't been impressed with her last-minute paper on the Salem witch-hunts.

"Now," Mr. Snibble was saying, "I'm returning your embarrassing critiques of *The Crucible* —" He paused, noticing Beth's hand in the air. "Yes, Ms. Fish?"

"It's not that I, you know, doubt you or anything, but you're saying the *entire* class tanked on the essay? All of us?"

It was unlike Beth to question a teacher — that was so Brianna's style. But since Cam couldn't break into her best bud's thoughts (Alex's was the only so-called mind she could read) she wasn't sure what Beth was doing — suggesting that Snibble rethink his marking system?

Their teacher didn't take offense. "Let's put it this way," he explained. "Everyone in this room could benefit by choosing an extra-credit project."

Beth pressed on, "No one got an A?"

Mr. Snibble sighed. "The only student who did well is Brianna Waxman, who doesn't seem to have joined us today. You wouldn't happen to know why, would you, Ms. Fish? You and she are good friends, are you not?"

Only the slightest tic gave Beth away. No way was she ratting out Bree. "Not really."

Snibble raised his eyebrows, gently baiting her. "You're not really good friends?"

Beth's freckled face reddened. Cam could tell she was embarrassed — and annoyed at being put on the spot. "We are friends. I'm just not all that sure why she's . . . uh . . . absent."

Mr. Snibble scanned the room. Had his gaze settled on Cam? "Does anyone know where Brianna is?"

No sooner was the question out of Snibble's mouth when, *Wham!* There it was, full-tilt intense and whiplash swift. Cam's eyes stung. Snibble's face faded. Everything around her blurred. A loud, insistent buzzing in her ears blocked out all other sounds. She was sweating and freezing at the same time. All of which meant just one thing. Camryn was about to have a vision.

She saw . . . a woman, a girl, someone she knew, yet did not recognize. The person was shivering in the snow, clutching her stomach, bent over, tears streaming down her face.

Then something happened that hadn't before: Cam could see through the eyes of the figure in the vision. She saw the back of a house. Brick, suburban, familiar . . . with a willow tree, a weeping willow. Whose house was it? Who was crying out in the cold?

As quickly as it had overtaken her, Cam's vision was gone. The snowbound stranger morphed into the familiar features of Beth Fish, now staring at her, a panicked look on her face. The buzzing in Cam's ears gave way to words.

"What's wrong?" Beth was scared.

"Ms. Barnes, are you ill?" Mr. Snibble was obviously concerned. Behind him, she heard the alarmed murmurs and embarrassed giggles of her classmates. How long had she been spaced?

"You're okay, right?" Beth's voice wavered. "You looked so out of it — and you're, like, sweating."

Cam blinked, pressed her palms on her desk for support, and tried to assure everyone that she was okay — though her throat was parched and her head pounded.

"Was it an attack of some sort?" Mr. Snibble was now asking.

Cam opened her mouth —

"She'll be fine!" The voice belonged to a girl charging into the classroom.

Alex.

She was at Cam's side in an instant. "I told you not to stay up studying all night," she scolded. "Mr. S?" Alex asked quickly, hoping to avoid the question of how she knew Cam needed her. "Would it be okay if I took my sister to the . . ."

"Nurse," he finished, relieved. "Yes, of course, Ms. Fielding. Good that you happened to be, ah, coincidentally walking by my classroom."

Alex nodded quickly, then helped her grateful sister up and out. As soon as they hit the girls' room, she handed Cam some aspirin. The visions she had were especially painful.

"How did you . . . ?" Cam started to ask, swallowing the pills while cupping her hand under the faucet for water — but she knew the answer before she finished asking the question.

"I heard something," Alex responded. "Someone

crying out for help. It was in the middle of that brain-boggling chem test and, dude, at first, I thought it was me, crying out for just one right answer."

In spite of feeling shaky, Cam managed a weak smile. "I told you — C, B, D, A. Anyway — tell me what you heard."

"Someone crying, choking, her teeth chattering," Alex answered. "'I'm so scared, so alone,' she was saying. 'No one understands. Why is this happening?'"

CHAPTER SEVEN
A PICTURE'S WORTH

"Do you think we should try to contact Karsh or Ileana?" Cam asked, zipping up her pink ski jacket and starting for home. Alex, with a ridiculous woolen cap that said MONTANA jammed on her head, fell into step with her.

They'd wanted to leave school sooner but that would have meant going to the nurse, and worse, contacting a parent. So they'd waited out the rest of the afternoon, in their separate classes, then dashed out together, when the dismissal bell rang.

"Too soon." Alex put the kibosh on sending a 911 to their guardians. "What would we say besides you had a vision and got a weird note?"

The sidewalk had been plowed, allowing only for a narrow path. In places, the twins had to walk single file.

"And you heard her voice," Cam reminded her sister. They'd heard Miranda speak just once before, just one sentence. This time, she hadn't sounded so soft and breathy.

"Her voice," Alex echoed, frowning. "It was . . . uh . . . how else can I put this? Whiny."

"Alex!" Cam whirled on her sister so quickly, she almost lost her footing. "You're a piece of work. Dissing your own mother before you've even met her."

They'd never seen a photo of Miranda, but who else could the woman in Cam's vision have been — the one who'd uttered the desperate pleas Alex had heard?

Uncomfortably, Alex shifted her backpack from one shoulder to the other. "I know I've heard that voice before — it just sounded different. Anyway, we're not in danger."

Alex was right. Karsh would probably tell them to pay attention to their instincts, not to be afraid, and to let their hearts and hunches guide their actions. As for Ileana? Did they really want to chance annoying the mercurial witch by requesting her presence in Marble Bay for "no reason"? Ileana's temper was a match for Lord Thantos's, Cam found herself thinking.

"At some point, we have to rely on ourselves," Alex said with resolve. "We can't always be calling them. Besides, we're getting more powerful all the time. There are some things we can do on our own."

They'd reached the house. "Well, at least we can be sure of one thing," Cam noted, wiping her boots on the mat. "Wherever Miranda is, it's snowy." Her hand froze on the doorknob. "Als, you don't think . . ."

"She's nearby? Down, girl. It's winter. Half the country is blanketed in snow. She could be anywhere in the northern hemisphere. But what about that palm tree — the one we picked out in the photo of Thantos? He was supposed to be at that clinic, right?"

"Could be artificial," Cam guessed. "Like in some hotel lobbies."

"The place is supposedly for celebs." Alex agreed, "It's probably totally plushed out."

"We're home!" Cam called as they went inside.

Silence greeted them.

A note left on the kitchen table explained, *Had to pick up a bolt of fabric for the Dennison job. Dad and I will be home around 6 with takeout.* There were individual memos scrawled on the bottom:

Cam: the dentist called to confirm your appointment.

Alex: the offer still stands to buy you a new winter jacket.

Dylan: No junk food! Call if you need anything. Love, Mom.

Love, Mom. As she bounded up the steps to log on to her e-mail, Cam thought of Emily writing that note, all conscientious and concerned; Emily, the sophisticated interior designer, who had decorated the hallway with her kids' framed kindergarten drawings; who made a fool of herself cheering for Cam at every soccer game all season long; who had accepted Alex into their family even though her daughter's identical twin was a daily reminder that Cam had another mother somewhere.

For some stupid reason, Cam began to well up with tears.

If Alex noticed, she didn't say anything. She did beat Cam to the computer, though, and booted it up.

Cam had mail, so did Alex. Only not the mail they were hoping for.

Deflated, Alex swung around to face her sister, confirming, "Still no message from *Starstuck*. They're ignoring us."

"Rude much?" Cam snuffled back her tears, pretending it was the weather that had made her eyes water and her nose red.

"That's why they call 'em rag-mags," Alex groused. "Maybe if we called back and said we were two-headed aliens who'd met Elvis in a galaxy far, far away . . . or that we've got a dog that can tell the future —"

"I've got a better idea," Cam said, her swollen eyes twinkling with sudden, mischievous inspiration. "Where'd we write down *Starstruck's* phone number?"

Alex was on it. "A little T'Witch trickery?"

Cam ran her fingers through her long thick hair, pulling it off her face, securing it in a scrunchie-held ponytail. "*Starstuck* wouldn't bother calling or writing back to Cam Barnes or Alex Fielding. So . . . who would they have to talk to?"

Instantly, Alex got it. The only debate was which T'Witch would actually make the call. Alex was faster — using her telekinetic power to draw the phone to her.

"Show-off." Cam folded her arms. "Put it on speaker."

Bypassing the voice-mail-o-rama, Alex hit "O" and waited until the operator said, "How may I direct your call?"

"I demand to speak to your photo editor immediately," Alex snapped.

"Who shall I say is calling?" the operator asked, bored.

"Tell him Alexandra DuBaer is on the phone, calling on behalf of Lord Thantos DuBaer."

The next voice they heard was gruff, irritable, but clearly trying to control its edginess. "Edwards. Photo Department. Who did you say this is?"

"Alexandra DuBaer, Lord Thantos's niece." Alex wavered only a tiny bit. "Are you the photo editor?"

"No, I'm Madonna," the man grumbled. "What can I do for you?"

"Lord Thantos"— Alex cleared her throat —"demands to know the name of the photographer who took his picture and to speak directly with him. Or her," she quickly added.

"Yeah, sure." Edwards gave a nasty snicker. "Look, whoever you are, I don't know what your game is, but no can do — even if I wanted to. Your photographer's not in —"

"When will he be back?" Alex was determined not to be brushed off.

"Never," Edwards cracked. "Does never work for you?"

Cam leaned into the speaker phone. "I don't think you want to incur Lord Thantos's wrath . . ."

Alex nudged her out of the way. "We need to talk to

the photographer. Our uncle . . . he . . . uh . . . wants to —"
Alex shrugged at Cam.

"Buy the picture!" Cam blurted.

The photo editor laughed. "Yeah, right. To frame it?"

"I don't see the humor in this, Mr. Edwards," Alex said bossily. "He wants to make sure it never gets published again. My uncle is a very private man."

"And rich," Cam added. "Money is not an object."

"Look, whoever you are," he said pointedly, "if you were really related to that egomaniacal money machine, you would know this. I can't sell you the picture."

"Can't? Or won't?" Cam asked dramatically. "Lord Thantos won't be happy —"

"He won't, won't he? Trust me on this, he's already made his displeasure known," Edwards said bitterly, and hung up.

Alex heard footsteps crunching in the snow outside.

"Dylan," Cam confirmed, without looking out the window. "Bum-osity. He's going to do twenty questions on the rumor that I got sick in class." As her brother slammed the front door and started up the stairs, she grabbed a book from her backpack, planted herself on the window seat, and pretended to be engrossed in her math book.

Alex propped her chemistry text on her pillow and belly-flopped onto her bed. Within a mo, she really was reading it. Already the first few questions on the test began to make sense.

"Chill," Cam advised her. "You had to come to my rescue. Olson will totally give you a makeup test."

"Let's pretend this is 'adult swim,'" Alex responded sourly. "How about a solid hour where you don't dive into my head? Anyway, I have no excuse for the first half of the test, which I was totally there for. It's not like I'm partying on the other coast, like your buds Bree and Kris."

Dylan sauntered into the room and their conversation, effortlessly. "Speaking of Kristen, what's up with her?" he asked. "Did she spend the weekend getting a personality transplant?"

Cam looked over at him. Alex rolled onto her back, clasping her hands behind her head.

"The sudden interest in my friends is inspired by . . . ?" Cam inquired.

Dylan dropped his messenger bag on the floor and made for Alex's guitar, formerly his, which was propped against the wall near her bed. "'Cause that girl has been acting too flaky lately."

"At the bowling alley, you mean?" Alex asked casually.

Dylan settled himself on the floor, bending over the

instrument intently, strumming it to see if it was in tune. "After that. On Sunday."

"Sunday?" Cam and Alex said simultaneously.

"You couldn't have seen Kristen on Sunday," Alex added.

Dylan's head jerked up. "Do you guys practice that? Saying stuff at the same time? Man!"

Cam swung off the window seat and settled herself in front of him. "Kristen's away with Bree. They're not supposed to be home until tomorrow."

"Well, they are. At least Kris is." Dylan's blue eyes stared directly into Cam's clear grays. "And little miss Minivan Gogh acted like she didn't know me."

"What happened, exactly?" Alex was sitting up now.

Dylan played a few chords. "When we finished boarding, Robbie's dad picked us up. He had some stuff to do in the city. We had a half hour to kill. Robs is making this mobile of the solar system for science, so we went into some arts and crafts place. Kristen, or her nervous clone, was at the checkout. I go, 'Hi,' she freaks. Dropped her stuff and bolted. Like I was Lord Voldemort. Weird, huh?"

Scale of 1–10. What are the chances he's mistaken? Alex sent her question silently to Cam.

Slim to none. He's known Kris — her whole family — for years.

Alex shrugged. "Maybe she got uninvited to Bree's party at the last minute."

Cam shook her head. "Doesn't account for her buggin' when Dylan spotted her. And why skip school? Extremely un-Kristen."

"Yo, Als," Dylan said, on to the next topic. "Wanna jam?"

"Sorry, dude, can't. I've got to . . ."

She was about to say "study," when Cam cut in. "Go ahead." Telepathically, she added, *We'll break it down later. There's nothing we can do right now, anyway.*

Alex closed her chem text and started out after Dylan. But not before she telegraphed Cam: *You're not getting rid of me so you can summon Karsh and Ileana, are you? I remind you, Camryn, they would not be pleased at the phone call we just made. Cool as it was!*

Cam rolled her eyes. *Simplify: I'm just getting rid of you.*

Cam waited until she heard two guitars and voices twanging next door. Then she grabbed her cell phone and dashed downstairs — hoping Alex would be too all about the music to listen in.

"Hello?" The voice on the other end was familiar.

Cam's breath caught in her throat. Why would she be nervous? "Is . . . uh . . . Kristen home? It's Camryn."

Samantha Hsu, Kris's older sister, paused. The question seemed to take her by surprise. "Try her cell phone," she advised.

Before Cam could continue, Samantha said, "Sorry, I have to go," and hung up.

Kristen answered right away. Thanks to caller ID, she knew who was calling — and didn't sound completely surprised to hear from Cam. "Cami, hey, what's up?"

"You tell me," Cam said. "Kris . . . where are you?"

"I can't really talk now," Kristen said, almost apologetically.

"You were in Boston on Sunday. You saw Dylan and bugged." Cam came clean. "So I know you're not in Los Angeles with Brianna. So why'd you blow off school today? What's going on?"

There was a long pause on the other end. "I'm sorry, Cam," Kris said. "I . . . I can't talk about it."

"Why not?" Cam looked up and saw Alex coming down the stairs.

"Emily just pulled into the driveway," her twin told her.

Cam turned as the front door opened. It was her mom, with a bolt of fabric under her arm, two shopping bags in one hand, and the mail in the other. Emily's face lit up automatically the moment she saw her daughter.

"I have a good reason," Kris was saying. "Camryn, listen, please don't call back."

"Kris, wait," Cam said, but her friend had hung up. Cam clicked off her cell phone and went to help Emily with her packages.

She sensed Alex watching them from the stairs, then heard her flame-haired sister's melancholy thoughts. It was the first time Alex had looked at them and realized how much Emily and Cam's relationship mirrored hers with Sara. Cam glanced up gratefully at her twin.

"Oh, this one's for you, both of you." Emily turned over a manila envelope. "No stamps. Someone must have shoved it into the mailbox." She smiled at Alex and handed the creased envelope to Cam, who was standing nearer. "Look at the address. Isn't that creative? The letters are all different styles and sizes."

Cam set down the bolt of fabric and hurried to her sister. The moment Emily left the hallway they tore open the envelope.

Inside was a sheet of paper with only eight words on it, some done in calligraphy, others printed in red in different urgent type styles:

If she doesn't **get help she could die!**

CHAPTER EIGHT
UNDER THE DOME: JUSTICE

The trial of Fredo DuBaer had begun.

Before each voting Council member was a computer on which he or she would register a secret verdict. The laptops, as Ileana had protested to Lady Rhianna, had all been donated by Lord Thantos. Ileana found herself frowning at them, as if they were the monstrous tracker himself.

"The computers," she whispered to Karsh. "What if Thantos has meddled with them? He's supposed to be a computer genius."

Karsh shook his head. "He's a genius at business. It was Aron who was brilliant at technology —"

From her perch at the People's bench, Ileana

glanced over at the surviving DuBaer brothers. What a bizarre pair they made — Fredo, short, slight, reedlike, his thinning dark hair slicked back with grease, a wispy goatee straggling from his pointy chin; Thantos, a looming, fearsome presence in a dark cape and hobnail boots, his beard thick and black as a moonless night.

In other circumstances, Karsh and Thantos might have been well matched against each other. They'd known each other all their lives, and both were men of intelligence who passionately believed in their arguments. But hapless Fredo had made such a tangled mess, it was doubtful that even a force like Thantos could persuade this Council of his brother's innocence.

Fredo, it turned out, had no alibis, no means of proving his innocence, and a pitiable parade of character witnesses. Ileana looked at the sad little group lined up behind the Accused's table. Five in all. Three of them wore the striped jumpsuits of convicted felons. One, a trembling young witch, worked for 3B, one of Thantos's computer brands. The last, a sad, shabby old warlock with gambling troubles, probably owed Thantos money. "Characters is right," she muttered to Karsh.

Ileana grew increasingly impatient as the circus parade of witnesses was called upon and led, one by one, through their predictable performances by Thantos.

Although Fredo grinned stupidly, as if he believed the praise their rehearsed testimony heaped upon him, the evidence against him was overwhelming. Punishing this bungling monster was so not the justice Ileana craved.

For her, this trial served only one satisfying purpose. It brought Thantos back to Coventry Island publicly, for the first time in years. He was the one who should have been tried and convicted! He had slain his brother Aron.

Thantos had never been formally charged, of course. He'd moved to the mainland, thus making sure no one would ever know what happened in those fateful predawn hours of late October, a decade and a half ago.

But he was here now. Finally! Could the Coventry Island Unity Council, the ruling body of the community, miss this golden opportunity to see Aron DuBaer's real killer finally pay for his ghastly crime?

Frowning defiantly, Ileana tugged at Karsh's sleeve. "There is no justice in this Council room," she whispered angrily.

"Patience." The old warlock gently removed Ileana's hand. "We've made our case against Fredo and, if I do say so myself, my closing argument was —"

"I don't mean Fredo's paltry offenses," Ileana interrupted, "I mean Thantos's. He is here, Karsh, on Coventry. Standing before the Unity Council. What better time to charge him with Aron's death?"

Karsh wasn't surprised at Ileana's demand. Personally, he was never completely convinced of Thantos's guilt. Many on the island, however, believed as Ileana did. This would not be a bad time to clear up the matter once and for all. Still, he couldn't bring himself to agree wholeheartedly with Ileana because he knew the pain such a public forum might cause her.

Thantos was wrapping his closing argument. Ileana seethed. She could barely stand to be in the same room with the murderous maniac, let alone forced to listen as he tried to convince the voting members of the Council that his brother was innocent — almost solely because he, the mighty Thantos DuBaer, said so!

When Thantos took his seat, Lady Rhianna announced, "The Unity Council now calls for a time-out in the proceedings. During this time, the Exalted Elders will study the transcript of this trial and then render their votes. The Accused" — she nodded at Fredo — "and the People" — she smiled fondly at Karsh — "are asked to vacate the amphitheater during this time. I will summon you when the Council has come to a decision."

Without a backward glance, Ileana led Karsh out of the domed arena. They settled down on a bench under one of Coventry's grand old evergreens. The day was unseasonably mild and many of the spectators who had been inside were strolling the grounds. They called out affectionate greetings to Karsh. Ileana nodded at them, but her fiery obsession had not abated.

Karsh tried to calm her. "Are you so sure —" he began.

"He killed Aron," she insisted, facing her guardian. "Aron, your friend, the twins' father, his own brother. Thantos murdered him in cold blood. Out of greed and jealousy. With Aron dead, Thantos became the sole owner of DuBaer Technologies."

"He is not the sole owner," Karsh corrected her. "Fredo also has an interest."

"Fredo doesn't count," Ileana persisted. "He's a tool of Thantos. Everyone knows that."

"They do with you shouting it like a banshee!" Karsh and Ileana looked up. A few feet above them, Lady Rhianna, plump yet graceful — and awe-inspiring with her magnificent wings unfurled — sailed toward the dome of the amphitheater. "I command you not to discuss this case outside of the courtroom," she warned them.

Ileana stood, but had no time to protest. For the moment Rhianna flew out of sight, two strangers appeared and jostled the young witch rudely.

"Beware," the taller one hissed, gripping Ileana's arm. "My father's punishment will be painless compared to yours."

"Let go of her," Karsh demanded. But the short, squat boy seized the old man's collar, almost strangling him in the process. "You. Karsh. Father of no one. You have already outlived your usefulness. Harm him and pay with your miserable life!"

Witches and warlocks all around them had stopped to stare at the ruckus. Almost wearily, Karsh reached into the pocket of his waistcoat, pulled out a pinch of herbs, and began mumbling an ancient incantation.

The stocky boy started suddenly to shrink. His large head grew small, his broad nose shortened, his lips pursed, and the thick fingers clutching the medallion turned into a tiny baby's hands that slipped from the ribbon.

Karsh was more astonished than the boy, who had become a feeble infant. It was not the spell he had intended. The second intruder, too, had been transformed — into a baby goat. Tiny and helpless, it stood on wobbly legs, bleating pitifully.

Karsh was stunned. He heard a flutter of wings and, looking up, saw his old friend Rhianna grinning mischievously. "Thank you, old friend," Karsh called to her. "Thank you for helping us. I . . . I tried to —"

"It was not I who performed that spell," Rhianna confessed. "Look around you. It was your friends. You are a much-loved warlock, Karsh. The witches of Coventry would not stand by and see you harmed."

Karsh, with Ileana holding his arm, turned to survey the group gathered around them. Among them Karsh recognized many fledglings, now grown, some now trackers themselves, whom he'd taught through the years. They had learned well, he thought gratefully.

"Who were those thugs?" Ileana asked.

"Tsuris and Vey," Lady Rhianna responded. "Fredo DuBaer's sons. They've lived with their mother on the mainland for most of their lives. They've returned for their father's trial."

As Rhianna sailed off, an unwelcome thought buzzed in Ileana's brain.

Karsh had told her that she was related to Camryn and Alexandra.

Fredo's wild sons, Tsuris and Vey, were also related to the twins. They were their cousins.

Was it possible that Fredo was Ileana's father?

She shuddered — not out of fear of what the reckless bullies would do, but at the repulsive possibility that they might be her brothers.

Karsh was bothered by something having nothing to do with Fredo's sons. "Your loathing of Lord Thantos runs deep, my child. Have you ever thought about why this is?"

Ileana did not speak out loud. She could not admit the possibility that had poisoned her thoughts recently — ever since she'd found out she was related to the twins. She wanted justice for Cam and Alex, she told herself. They were, after all, her responsibility now.

Typically, they needed help — though, thank goodness, they hadn't called for it yet. They were trying to track down their mother. As if fifteen-year-old fledglings could succeed where seasoned witches and warlocks had failed.

Yes, but none were Miranda's children. Karsh read her mind and responded.

At least they know who their parents were! she silently telegraphed back, hating the shrill sound of her own thoughts.

And so shall you, in time, Karsh promised.

How she wished he were her true father. In every way but biology he was. The wise old tracker, whose hair had already been white the day he found her, had done everything for her: fed, clothed, and sheltered her; schooled her brilliantly in the ways of the craft; persuaded the Unity Council to appoint her guardian — the youngest witch ever promoted to such a position — of the infant twins; and instilled in her a strong, if troublesome, sense of goodness and justice, though he hadn't done as well with courtesy and tolerance.

Ileana never doubted that Karsh loved her. And that there was little he would refuse her. She had forced him to admit her kinship with Camryn and Alexandra. Long ago she'd found out from him that her mother died in childbirth. The only thing Karsh wouldn't do was reveal the name of her father.

Karsh and Ileana made their way back to the vast, circular building. The message had been sent telepathically: The Exalted Elders had made their decision. The verdict was in.

Walking to the People's table, they passed Thantos and Fredo. The tall, evil tracker ignored them, but Fredo, his swamp-green eyes glistening with hatred, grinned at Karsh. "So you've met my boys," he whispered proudly in his grating, high-pitched voice. "Little demons. They're utterly unpredictable."

Ileana followed Fredo's glance to the highest tier of the round auditorium. There in the shadowy rafters were the boys who had accosted them during the break, Fredo's sons, returned to their human forms. Their father's glare was mild compared to the look Tsuris and Vey bestowed on her.

Ileana quickly turned away from them.

At that moment, the dome darkened. The chattering grew hushed. All eyes faced the center of the arena, where three gilded chairs sat empty, except for plush velvet cushions. A spotlight fell on one of the chairs. In a puff of pink smoke, a magnificent Asian child appeared — a girl so young her feet barely reached the edge of the cushion.

The auditorium grew animated. Whispers of "Fan, it's Lady Fan" reached Ileana's ears. In a moment's time, the child aged from two to twelve to twenty-two; from a delicate girl to a petite middle-aged woman to a distinguished Elder to, finally, Fan, the wizened crone with dark shining eyes and tiny wrinkled hands.

As the aged Lady Fan dipped her head, acknowledging the applause of the coven, the spotlight shifted to a second empty chair. A burst of green smoke gave way to a gulping toad that quickly grew into a greenish, rubbery-limbed man who became an olive-skinned old warlock with long white hair, recognizable as the doddering Lord Grivveniss.

The clapping had barely subsided when a great golden gust swirled on the empty center chair. All quieted in anticipation. And Ileana noticed a tender smile creep across Karsh's white face as he stared expectantly at Lady Rhianna's spotlighted throne.

Fire leaped from the cushion. Tongues of heat

spread outward. From the center of the blaze a magnificent bronze dragon materialized; the dancing flames became its golden wings. The dragon spun once, twice, three times — at the third turning, Rhianna's buxom form burst forth, aglow with power, wisdom, and joy.

Settling herself into the chair, her wings folded inside a golden cape, the brown-skinned leader of the Unity Council raised her plump arms triumphantly. And the dome exploded with pleasure.

One cheer boomed above the others. Ileana didn't have to look to know it was Thantos's. But she did glance over at the Accused's table. And, yes, the dark tracker was admiring Rhianna's transformation. Fredo, too, was grinning — but not at Lady Rhianna. He was gleefully looking just behind and just above the bench where Karsh and Ileana sat.

If he were reading her mind, he would have realized she'd long ago lost interest in his trial and that this was the moment she'd decided to stand and formally accuse Thantos. She would keep silent no longer. She scrambled to her feet.

"Wait!" a scratchy voice suddenly whispered in her ear. "They may need you." Startled, she whirled, to see Fredo's chunky son, Vey. "Apolla and Artemis may be in desperate trouble. And you won't be able to rush to their aid, will you?"

"Not while you're busy betraying their family!" Tsuris leaned forward, behind Karsh, a shock of dark hair falling over his slitted eyes. "Our pretty little cousins may cry out for help. In vain, alas, in vain! No one to answer their pathetic pleas." Vey giggled cruelly. "So you must choose," he said. "Which is more important to you: seeing my father destroyed, plotting to soil my uncle's reputation with your ruinous accusation — or saving the twins?"

CHAPTER NINE
THE TRIP

Cam was out of breath as she raced up the snowy path to the top of the hill. She felt like a tuning fork tingling with anticipation. She and Alex were about to attempt extreme magick. "Tell me we're not really doing this," she said, elated.

"We're not really doing this," Alex deadpanned. A step behind her twin, she stopped and took a deep breath, partly to get calm, partly to get ready. Because she wasn't.

She reviewed why the drastic step they were about to take was necessary.

One, she reminded herself, the anonymous notes warning that their mother was in grave danger and needed them.

Two, Cam's vision of the desperate woman weeping in the snow. Who else could it have been but Miranda?

Three, the photo of Thantos visiting a clinic. Clinic, sanitarium, asylum, nuthouse, cuckoo's nest — whatever you called it, it was a practically perfect place to stash someone who had gone crazy.

"But why would he keep her there? Why not kill her?" Cam checked in.

"Simple," Alex said, sounding surer than she felt. "To get at us, of course. We're supposed to develop into these genius witches, right? Take after our parents and all. And Ileana's always saying that Thantos wants to get us on his side, use our powers to —"

"Get richer and more powerful himself," Cam offered.

"So he kept her alive just to tempt us — or, like, blackmail us into working with him."

"I'm getting a headache," Cam complained.

"Are you having another vision?" Alex asked hopefully.

"No, just this monster migraine from thinking about our messed-up family!"

For the first time that morning, Alex laughed. "Okay, dude, let's do this thing." She glanced at her watch. It was still early. Emily and Dave would be thinking that they were on their way to school. Never guessing that Cam, pretending to be Emily, had called the attendance office asking that "her daughters" be excused for the day due to stomach flu. Or that, for the price of four new CDs, Dylan was down with the caper and had sworn not to rat them out.

Tuesday morning, Cam thought, and here they were at the highest point in Mariner's Park, standing under the sacred old oak tree. From the mound in which its deep roots burrowed, the entire U-shaped, boat-lined harbor was visible below. But Cam had never come for the view. It was the tree itself that had drawn her. She'd always known there was something special about it. Recently she'd discovered that her instincts were right. It was beneath the ancient oak, fifteen years ago, that Karsh had entrusted her to David Barnes. Alex was the only other person who knew the importance of this place. If they were going to make their scheme work, this was the spot to start.

The spell was called the Transporter. Accomplished witches and warlocks who knew how to use it were instantly carried from one location to another. Cam and Alex had tried it only once before — and had wound up not just transporting themselves, but calling up a traveler from the past!

"And that time," a nervous Alex reminded Cam, "we only had to go across town."

Cam, psyched, unzipped her backpack. "I don't remember there being a limit on how far it could take you."

She hoped she was right about that.

They needed to find the "intrepid" photographer — Als had looked it up; "intrepid" meant brave, fearless — who took the picture of Thantos leaving the celebrity clinic. He could tell them where their uncle had been. Plan B: They'd wheedle the guy's whereabouts out of that photo editor, Edwards, who had to know more than he'd told them over the phone.

Mission? Rated D — for Doable.

Speed bump? *Starstruck's* offices were three thousand miles away, in Carlston, California.

Take the next jet west? Not an option. Get Dave and Emily to finance the one-day round-trip? Not this millennium. The Barneses were so not Eric Waxman, who'd send his daughter a first-class ticket on a whim.

Thinking of Brianna made Cam uneasy. There was something so off about that whole L.A. party thing. Cam's convo with Kristen had proved it. But what was really going down? Ouch! Too much thinking again.

"Yo, Cam, we are now leaving Six Pack land. We didn't cut school so you could moon over your buds." Alex had tapped into her overloaded brain. "Oh, speaking of buds — as in flowers — did you get the mugwort?"

Cam pulled a handful of scraggly dried weeds from

her backpack. "Herbs in the 'Burbs had one bunch left," she crowed. "And I've got the candles, crystals, and incense."

"Incantation right here." Alex waved the sheet of notebook paper on which she'd copied the spell. "Now all we need is for our heads and hearts to be in the right place." She was quoting from Ileana's *Little Book of Spells.*

"Right," Cam agreed, taking out the candles. She'd bought the ones in jars, to shield them from the wind. "And a passion to do good."

"Whatever." With a twig she'd found, Alex drew a circle in the snow, wide enough to surround Cam and herself.

Placing the candle glasses at the four points of the circle, Cam instructed, "Face east."

"I know." Alex knelt inside the circle. "Toward the water."

As Alex lit the candles, Cam sprinkled the dried mugwort flakes around them, then handed the dregs of the herb and one of the crystals to Alex. "Got passion?" she teased, stepping into the circle.

"Got all the time in the world?" Alex shot back, pulling her sister down into the snow. "Just get it over with. We need to do this and get home."

Holding hands, they read the incantation together.

As they recited the final lines, "*Good magick like air and water flow, Transport me body and spirit now,*" snow began to churn about them. The icy wind seemed to whip away their words. And then they were swirling inside a spinning darkness.

In an instant Cam knew something had gone very, very wrong. "We're not in Kansas anymore, Toto." The line from *The Wizard of Oz* reverberated in Cam's head as she slowly gazed around. She was completely lost . . . and alone.

A trio of "nots" flew through her addled brain. She was not inside the offices of *Starstuck;* the spell had not worked; and she had so not prepared for this possibility.

"I will not freak out. I will not freak out," she chanted, trying to slow her thudding heart. Repeated calls for Alex — out loud and telepathic — went unanswered.

"Okay, I may be scared," she confessed, hoping the sound of her own voice would reassure her, "but I'm not helpless." She paused. "I'm a witch. Maybe not full-fledged yet. But I can handle stuff."

A wet and furry, long-tailed, gray creature brushed her leg as it scurried by. Cam shrieked and leaped back as the trembling rat disappeared down a sewer grate.

"Stuff that doesn't include rodents," she amended.

Looking around, she saw warehouselike buildings surrounded by empty parking lots. She was in some kind of industrial area. But what state, what city?

It was still dark. She'd probably gone west, where the day hadn't yet dawned. And south, as it was warmer here, no snow or wind, just air thick with an eerie silence. The area was run-down, deserted, creepy. The single streetlight still working cast a pale green glow over a nightmare setting, where danger hid and pounced.

What next, what now?

Hello! Her cell phone! She plucked it out of her pocket.

No service were the words across the screen.

Cam stopped suddenly. There was a break in the silence. She heard the unmistakable sounds of footsteps. People! She was either saved — or sunk. Using her zoom-lens eyesight, she found them.

A block away, diagonally across a wide street, a couple was headed toward her. The one walking faster was a tall, stocky man wearing a baseball cap. He carried a suitcase in each hand. Cam focused in on his face. Did he look dangerous? More like desperate, she decided. He gnawed on his bottom lip; his deep-set eyes darted constantly as if he were fearfully looking out for something or someone.

A few steps behind him, a worried woman holding a sleeping child hurried to keep pace with the man.

Waving, Cam was about to shout, "Hello!" but the word never left her throat. Still a block away from the worried strangers, Cam stopped dead in her tracks and whirled around.

Behind her. It would come from that direction. . . . Her eyes began to sting viciously, her vision went blurry. An icy chill wracked her. And she saw: a big black car skidding around the lamppost corner, swerving wildly toward the frightened family.

Two guys were in the high front seat, one tall, the other short and squat. The tall boy, who was driving, pushed back a shock of dark hair that had fallen over his eyes. His face was animated by a wild grin.

The passenger next to him turned suddenly as if he'd felt Cam's eyes on him. He leered at her, then let out a spine-tingling laugh.

The boys from the bowling alley, Cam realized. They were aiming deliberately at the frightened couple and their child. But why? And when would their car turn the corner? How much time did she, and they, have? Five minutes, ten at the most. It would happen . . .

Now!

She burst from the vision back to reality, shouting, "Watch out! Watch out!"

The woman clutching the baby stopped, terrified. "Don't cross the street!" Cam warned as the wary mother stood at the edge of the curb, searching the darkness for her.

Suddenly, the man stuck one of the suitcases under his arm and reached to pull his wife forward. "Come on!" he hollered impatiently. "There's no time to stop. I told you, he said they're looking for me!"

Cam raced toward them, holding up her hand, yelling, "Wait! Don't go! A car is coming." But the man's frantic shouting drowned her out. "Molly, come on!"

And then it was too late.

They were off the curb, rushing across the broad boulevard.

In desperation, Cam clutched her sun necklace, focusing hard on the threesome. A nanosecond of doubt held her back. Would it work alone, without Alex's moon charm? Could she save them all by herself? "Help," she whispered. "Tell me what to do. I don't know what to do. . . ."

Just then, the woman stopped walking and looked straight at Cam.

"Don't," Cam began weakly, but as the sun charm began to heat in her hand, her voice became sure and strong. "*Spirits who protect and love the innocent and helpless,*" she chanted, holding the frightened woman's gaze. *"Save from harm all those you judge kind of heart and selfless."*

A mask seemed to fall over the woman's taut face. As if in a trance, she slipped her hand out of the man's and stepped back onto the curb.

Cam set her sight on the man, but his cap shaded his eyes. She could not make contact with him. "Stop," she wanted to shout. Instead, it was the woman's voice that cried out, "Stop. Elias, wait. Come back. Come here!"

He was in too much of a hurry, too frightened. Cam's scream seemed to blend with the wailing of the woman and her wakened baby. That was all she remembered. That, and wishing Emily were there, to hold and comfort her.

She was wakened by the polar opposite of nurturing warmth.

"I can't leave you alone for a minute, can I? This is what I get for trusting you!" Ileana!

Cam had never been so relieved to hear that icy voice, to see the haughty expression, the jutting cheekbones and windblown golden hair, to see the dangerously flashing gray eyes of Ileana staring at her.

"What are you doing here?" It was a rhetorical question, asked as Ileana opened her cape and signaled for the trembling, blubbering Cam to wrap herself inside it. She pretended not to hear the fledgling's tale of a man being run down by two terrifying boys, how she'd seen it coming and had not been able to save him. How she could only help the woman with the baby —

"Do you think this is all I have to do?" the imperious witch interrupted. "Keep bailing you out of trouble? I'm in the middle of what may be the most important trial in the history of Coventry Island and you force me to choose between you and seeing justice done!"

Cam tried to explain, but Ileana wanted the answer to only one question: "Where's your sister?"

CHAPTER TEN
ALEX'S EXCELLENT ADVENTURE

Exactly as it had happened before, a sharp breeze set the candle flames flickering, then swirled around Alex, enclosing her in a funnel of whirling wind. When she opened her eyes, it took her a moment to realize that she was inside an office, surrounded by cubicles, computers, file cabinets. Photos and wacky headlines shared a huge bulletin board with schedules and dates.

Excellent! The Transporter had worked! She was inside *Starstruck*'s headquarters. Even better, she was exactly where she'd wanted to be: in the photo department, which was very quiet. On California time, it was too early for anyone to have arrived at work.

"Dude!" Alex spun around to slap palms with Cam.

"We're in — we did it!" She was about to say, "You the girl," only Cam wasn't there. Alex called out, "Camryn! I'm in here, in the photo department! This rocks!"

No answer. She shrugged. Okay, Cam must've landed in another part of the building. Sending a telepathic message, Alex figured her sister would find her — meanwhile, there was no time to waste. Edwards wasn't in yet, but the picture they'd come for probably was.

Where to begin? The photo honcho's office would be a good place to start. But where was that? Main dude? Biggest office.

The nameplate read ALVIN D. EDWARDS, DIRECTOR OF PHOTOGRAPHY. Alex opened the door. Ole Alvin commanded a spacious suite. But it reeked!

The ventilation hadn't kicked on yet and the windows in Edwards's messy workplace were sealed and strictly for the view. The office was seriously cluttered. Filing cabinets banked two walls. On his humongous desk, practically hiding the computer and the multiline phone, were piles of files, photo loops, notes, random supplies, and, big surprise, crumpled coffee cups and cellophane wrappings, complete with morsels of muffins, doughnuts, and cream-filled mystery cakes that even Dylan, the ultimate junk foodie, would reject.

Alex started with the cabinets. Luckily, Edwards alphabetized. She worked her way from A for Aliens to Z for Zilch. Which is what she came up with: There were no files for Thantos or DuBaer anywhere.

She attacked the litter on Edwards's desk, stopping every once in a while to listen for Cam or zap her another message. No go.

An hour later, Alex had rifled through hundreds of prints and slides but had not found the one she was looking for.

Nor had Cam arrived.

Dejectedly, Alex plopped into Edwards's chair. The only place she hadn't searched was the top drawer of his desk. It might contain a random picture or two. Wrong. It was Edwards's junk drawer. Among pens, stickies, paper clips, and rubber bands were half-eaten candy bars, enough crumbs to host an ant convention, a shriveled, dripping peach, and a blackened dead banana. Someone get this guy a Dustbuster and a fumigator!

Wrinkling her nose, Alex pushed aside the leftovers and reached into the back of the drawer. She came up with a handful of laminated badges, press passes for employees. She flipped through them. Neither the people in the pictures nor the names rang a bell.

She was about to toss them back in the drawer when a familiar, sickening feeling washed over her like a tsunami. Her senses sharpened as she honed in on something far away. She heard: screeching tires, busted glass, horrified shrieks. "No! No! Elias!" And then, a baby crying.

Alex jumped up and looked out the window. Daylight was dawning, but the street below was peaceful, no cars, no screaming people. The crash hadn't happened there. Well, where then? Could there be some connection between the ID badge in her hand and the terrible sounds of an accident? She sat back in Edwards's chair and checked out the mug shot. A thick-necked man in a backwards baseball cap. The name tag said . . .

"Alexandra DuBaer, I presume."

Alex froze — and looked straight up into the beady eyes of a man so mountainous he filled the door frame. She hadn't heard him coming: The car crash had obscured all other sounds. This dude was mammoth. And snarling. She was so busted.

Lamely, she went for a quip. "And you would be . . . um . . . Madonna?"

Edwards was ferociously unamused. His eyes bored into her. "You've got some nerve," he growled. "You little punk. Think you can just break in here and go through my stuff?"

Alex calculated the distance between herself and the doorway. Edwards was about to pop a vein. If he took three steps toward her, she'd be toast.

"What do you think you're doing?" he demanded.

"Helping." Pathetic much? It was all she could think of to buy time.

"Helping yourself straight into juvie — by the looks of you, exactly where your kind belongs!" he barked at her. "Breaking and entering, trespassing, stealing. I'd call security, but it's going to be much more satisfying to haul you out myself."

He came at her. So did an idea.

Alex pictured the rotten banana in the desk drawer. Could she act quickly enough to send the squishy, revolting thing, sliding across the floor? It wasn't much, but . . .

"Whoa . . . Ow! What the . . . ?!" The big man slid into a skid, then went down hard. But he wasn't down to stay — and, unlike the bowling alley bozo, Edwards seemed intent on causing major bodily harm.

From his flat-out position on the floor, he glared at her. "You little freak! You're gonna be sorry you ever set foot in this office."

Time was so not on Alex's side. Edwards would be up in a minute. Other people would be here soon —

She could run — but . . . nah.

She needed to know the photographer's name.

Where was Cam? Her sister could stun people, fasten them to the floor with a stare, dazzle them into confessing what they didn't want to. If there was ever a time Alex needed those skills, this was it.

But she was alone, helpless . . . except for her wits, her necklace . . . and the crystal and herb flakes Cam had given her!

Alex took them out of her pocket and tossed what was left of the mugwort at Edwards.

The photo editor laughed. "That's your weapon? Parsley?"

Clutching her half-moon necklace in one fist and the crystal in the other, Alex recited the Truth Inducer incantation:

"*Free him*," she said, feeling her half-moon charm begin to warm. *"Free Alvin Edwards . . . from doubt and shame."*

The laughter caught in his throat. He stared at her as though she were crazy.

"Let us win his trust . . . And lift his blame."

"Girlie, Ms. DuBaer, or whatever your name is," Edwards said with no trace of anger, "you're barking up the wrong guy. That picture came in by e-mail from a freelancer."

McCracken — the name on the ID badge. Alex remembered the one she'd been holding when she heard the phantom car crash.

"We published the picture," the editor went on, "saved it in our cyber files. And it's gone. Believe me, only a big-time computer hacker — a guy like your uncle — could have cracked our system and deleted it — but someone did. That picture you're looking for is history."

Edwards lay back on the floor of his office. He put his arms under his head and stared up at the ceiling.

"I tried to find McCracken after you called," he finally said. "He must have changed his screen name like he changed his address. The check we mailed him came back stamped 'Moved. No Forwarding Address.' And get this, it was his biggest score yet," Edwards said admiringly. "Something must've spooked him."

Or someone, Alex thought.

This whole trip had been a failure. Her heart sank. No photo, no photographer. And no idea where Cam was.

"She's at home, where she belongs — as do you!" Ileana, boiling mad, sailed into the office, glaring at Alex.

Edwards's eyes bugged at the sight of the exquisite velvet-draped witch. He lifted his head to watch her. Ileana sighed impatiently and waved her hand over his supine body. His head fell back with a thud, eyes rolling, unconscious. Daintily, she stepped over him. "Let's go," she grumbled at Alex. "Your timing stinks!"

CHAPTER ELEVEN
THIS JUST IN

Ileana hung around just long enough to tear into them.

"The Transporter is off-limits to you! None but the initiated may use it." She stalked around the Barneses' family room, cape flaring, stiletto heels clicking on the polished wood floor, while Cam nervously toyed with the spell book Ileana had left them. "Which you two" — whirling dramatically, she pointed at Cam and Alex — "are not. And will not be until your sixteenth birthdays — if you survive until then!"

Before they could protest, or remind her that it was she who'd given them the book, Ileana snatched it back, adding, "As your guardian, I forbid you to use that spell again. Do not think about trying to find that photographer. Or, for that matter, your mother."

Cam, shaken from the hit-and-run, was curled up in a corner of the couch. Her cell phone rang, but she didn't bother answering it. She only whimpered, "You don't know what it's like. Not knowing if one of your real parents is dead or alive. It can be —"

"Frustrating, maddening, all consuming?" Ileana's searing eyes softened briefly with compassion. "I have some small experience in the area," she assured them. "Now," she continued, pausing to clear her throat, "if, against all odds and evidence, Miranda is alive — big if — I will be the one to find her. End of story."

She turned away abruptly, as if to prove the conversation was over. But, Alex suspected, it was her thoughts Ileana wanted to hide from them.

She wasn't fast enough.

What they just accomplished is amazing. Karsh was right.

Alex caught every glowing word.

Together, they're powerful beyond imagination. But they need so much help. Without humility, education, discipline, and the wisdom of an ancient community to guide them, their talents can be corrupted; their gifts become their downfall. Bright as they are, Ileana told herself, *they cannot win against Thantos! They*

*may not even be capable of besting Fredo's wild boys,
who were probably sent by their miserable uncle to
taunt the twins. The very idea that Thantos pretends to
know where Miranda is, that he visits her, is probably a
trap. He must be stopped. Now!*

With a regal toss of her flaxen hair, Ileana announced, "I'm off."

"Wait." Alex sprang from the high-backed chair
she'd been parked in. "You're supposed to help us. I
mean, if you don't believe Miranda is alive, then tell us
what the notes mean. Someone's been sending us messages about Miranda. We think they're from Thantos. Can
you at least confirm or deny?"

Ileana heaved a dramatic sigh. "Fine. I'll grant you one
more minute of my valuable time. Make the most of it."

Alex darted up to their room and was down a moment later with the two anonymous notes they'd received.

Ileana read them, turned them over, sniffed at the
paper they'd come on. "You think this is Thantos's work?
You must be joking," she said finally. "Not even the most
primitive witch or warlock would communicate in this
coarse fashion. This," she said, tossing the pages back to
Alex, "is a joke from one of your infantile friends."

Cam was depressed. The feeling was new to her
and unwelcome. They'd messed up the spell and, in ad-

dition to not being any closer to finding Miranda, it had cost an innocent man his life.

Now Ileana was gone and Cam's brain was stuck on replay. Alex had ended up in the right place, but left without a single lead. Both the picture and the dude who took it were MIA. Ileana and probably Karsh were furious with them.

If only that was the worst of it. Not even.

That would come when Emily Barnes got home.

Cam's mild-mannered mom was a wreck. Coat askew, with hat hair, makeupless, she stomped toward the front door in high heels made for stylish strolling. "Wreck" morphed into "wrath" when she realized the twins were in the family room. Tossing down her fuzzy hat, blue eyes blazing, she laced into them.

"You're here? You're home? I called everywhere! No one knew where you were! I called your cell phone five minutes ago!"

Cam gulped. She wanted to say something, but her mom was just warming up. No way would she get a word in here.

"You cut school! One of you called and pretended to be me — how could you lie like that?" With each sentence, Emily's voice seemed to go up an octave. Had Dylan gotten trapped into confessing? Cam wondered — but not for long. Emily promptly solved that mystery.

"The dentist called!" As if she'd just read Cam's mind, Emily railed, "He wanted to see if you could come in during lunch today instead of after school. I called you. When I couldn't get through, I tried the school office. Imagine my surprise — and embarrassment — to find out that I had called earlier this morning!" Cam's stomach fell, landing with a splash in a puddle of guilt.

"Where were you? Your father and I were worried sick! Didn't you even think about that?" Emily stopped pacing and stood with her hands on her hips, glaring at them.

We didn't think we'd get caught, Alex was thinking.

Emily stared right at her. "Or didn't it occur to you that you might get caught!"

Alex's jaw dropped. Had the woman read her mind? Well, if Alex returned the favor, she'd probably catch Emily thinking: This kind of thing never happened before Alex got here!

She knew she was being paranoid. Emily was just as ticked at Cam, maybe even more so since Princess Perfect never got in trouble, Alex thought sourly, until, oops, trouble came to her.

Quietly, Cam said, "Mom? Just one thing. It wasn't Alex. It was me. If you have to blame one of us, blame me. And also . . . Mom? We won't do it again."

If Emily heard her, she didn't show it. She'd spent hours panicked at the thought that something awful had happened to them. She was too worked up now to turn the switch to cool down. In fact, she was just warming up.

"If I find out you involved your brother in this . . ."

Alex fell back onto the opposite end of the sofa where Cam had curled up again. Without glancing at each other, they suffered in polite silence through Emily's tirade. It finally ended with, "I can't wait to hear why you did this and, giving you the benefit of the doubt, I'm assuming there's a very good reason."

Of course there was. Just none Emily would believe. In fact, there was nothing they could say to Dave, either, when he arrived home a few minutes later. David Barnes, who knew Karsh, who knew the importance of protecting the girls — though not specifically why or from what — was as angry as Cam had ever seen him. Clearly, he was severely shaken by what might have happened to them, and of failing as a father and a guardian.

"But, Dad," Cam began.

"We're so sorry, uh . . ." Alex thoughtfully omitted "dude" from the end of the sentence.

Emily sighed deeply and glanced at her husband. His usually smiling, mustached face was stern and ashen.

Cam looked at Alex, who nodded knowingly.

They were so grounded.

Grounded at home. Detention at school. Alex's life was nothing if not well balanced. Twin punishments for only one twin.

Of course, cutting was not exactly Alex's first infraction at Marble Bay High. But it was Cam's trouble debut, so she got off scot-free —

Unless you counted the Six Pack's slam book of snooping. Beth, Kristen, Bree, Sukari, and Amanda were all over the leader of the pack to spill, dish, get down, and tell them where she and her twin had been. In the end they had to settle for Cam's lame excuse: "Als and I just had stuff to do."

Everyone swallowed it but Beth.

All morning long, Cam's curly-haired bff pestered her. "What happened? Why didn't you answer my calls, my IMs? Were you at the doctor? Did it have to do with your . . . you know . . . mini space-out the other day?"

Cam pressed assurances on Beth, but nothing worked. In third period Spanish, her rangy bud played the I-know-you-better-than-anyone, I-know-when-something's-wrong card. And then, her voice laced with real fear, she asked softly, "You're not, like, sick or anything, are you?"

Cam caved. On the way to lunch, she pulled Beth

into an empty classroom for a sidebar — which, before Cam said a word, viciously freaked her freckled friend. "Oh, no! You need privacy. There's something wrong with you. This is the part where you tell me —"

"Where I tell you again what I've been telling you: 98.6, good to go, and ready to rumble!" With a deep sigh, Cam leaned against the blackboard, one knee jutting out, heel pressed against the wall. "There's just some stuff I'm dealing with," she began. "If I tell you, you've so got to swear not to breathe a word of it. It's about our . . ." Cam hesitated. It was hard for her to say "real mother" to Beth, who considered Cam's house a second home and Emily a second mom.

But Beth, dealing with her parents' recent separation, was ahead of her. "It's a family thing, right?"

Cam knew she'd have to tread carefully. Still, having a confession session with her best and oldest friend — like going bowling, flirting, pigging out on pizza at Pie in the Sky — felt so good, so right, so every girl.

Beth knew nothing about Cam's witch heritage, about Karsh, Ileana, Coventry Island, Thantos, or freaky Fredo. But everyone knew that Cam and Alex had been adopted. So spending a day searching for their birth mother wouldn't seem all that strange.

Especially since they'd recently received anonymous notes saying that their mystery mom needed them.

Beth exhaled and ran her hand through her thick mass of curls. "Wow. That's really scary. Your par — I mean, Emily and Dave don't know?"

"No. And that's why you can't tell anyone," Cam repeated.

Beth made a zipping motion across her lips. "You've got it." Then she smiled and shrugged. "Keeping your secrets is a full-time job. So, is there anything you want me to do besides that? I mean, you know, like in the old days —"

Before Alex, she meant. Before Alex had come into the picture, Beth was Cam's other self, the girl who knew what she was thinking before she said it. Not the way Alex, with her brain-picking hyperhearing, did, but instinctively, naturally, just from being together and liking the same things and each other.

Impulsively, Cam hugged Beth Fish. "You are totally the best," she said as they walked back out into the corridor. "I know you'd do anything for me and, like, I hope you know I'm there for you, too."

"One hundred fifty percent," Beth agreed. They walked in silence toward the lunchroom. They walked past the friendship art display. "That's Kristen's creation." Beth nodded at the strange collage. "So what do you think, which one's Kris and which one's Bree?" she joked.

Cam's eyesight blurred. Oh, no, not here, not

around Beth again, she thought, seeing, distantly, the slim woman on her knees in the snow, anguished, rocking back and forth and crying. Beth will think I'm sick and freaking. Was there a way to stop a vision? Was there an incantation or herb to bring her back from the brink of unconsciousness?

"Okay, then," Beth was whispering happily as Cam's sight sharpened again. They were standing in front of the lunchroom doors, about to go inside. "When do you want me to look at the notes? I think you're right. Maybe a fresh pair of eyes, a different perspective. Who knows? I might see some clue you haven't."

A wall of sound greeted them as they entered the school cafeteria. After yesterday's horror, Cam was grateful to be back, safe and all about the buzz.

At the Six Pack table, Brianna, draped in an oversized Polo sweatshirt, was holding court. Slender fingers flying to punctuate her sentences, she regaled everyone in earshot with tales of glitzy L.A., the *In Style*-worthy casa de Waxman, and how, of all the stars at her party, Brice Stanley was the nicest. They'd gotten totally chummy.

Wonder if Ileana knows? Alex, barred from leaving the school building as she usually did during lunch, telegraphed Cam, who slid onto the bench next to Beth.

Let her have her fun, Cam responded. *I don't think a fifteen-year-old is much competition for our goddess.*

Especially this one. If Bree had gotten one ray of California sunshine, it didn't show. She looked paler than ever. She looked, Cam found herself thinking, like the wailing woman in her vision.

Brianna's cheery chirping did not improve Alex's mood. Bree sounded like a sparrow on a sugar high. One weekend in Hollywood, and *poof!* The mouth of Marble Bay was back, too hip for the cosmos. It didn't hurt that Marco, a few tables away, had to eat his lunch sitting on some geriatric butt cushion — due to his unfortunate collision with the bowling alley floor.

"Hey, where's Kris?" Beth asked, unwrapping her sandwich. "Don't tell me she fell in love with L.A. and decided to stay."

Without hesitating, Bree responded, "She's here. She came back with me Monday night. But she did fall in love at my party. She's probably in the computer lab, e-mailing Josh Hartnett as we speak."

Cam nearly choked on her alfalfa sprouts and peanut butter sandwich. Coughing, she cast a sidelong glance at Alex, who rolled her eyes.

Dylan had seen Kris on Sunday — a fact Ms. Hsu had not bothered to deny. Deduction: She'd probably never gone to L.A. at all. But why would Brianna lie about it?

No one seemed to have caught Cam and Alex's

silent exchange. Beth sniffed her sandwich and wrinkled her nose. "Anyone want to trade? One more tuna sandwich and I turn into . . ."

"A Fish?" Sukari chortled at her own joke. "I'll swap. If you can stand ham and cheese with an overdose of mayo. But," she added, eyeing the rest of Beth's lunch, "sweeten the deal. Throw in the cupcake."

"Done," Beth said, switching lunch bags.

"Yuck," Bree commented, staring at the food exchange. "I mean," she quickly laughed, "tuna for ham and cheese — it's like switching seats on the *Titanic*."

Licking the chocolate frosting off the cupcake, Sukari threw Bree a look, then eyed Alex. "We get our chem papers back next period. I'm thinking I did between an A and an A minus. You?"

Alex motioned with a thumbs-down. "No thinking required. I totally tanked."

Sukari shrugged. "Olsen might let you take a make-up test." Suke turned to Brianna suddenly. "Hey, you were absent that day, too. You guys could probably take a makeup together — be study buddies. How cute would that be?" she teased.

Brianna's eye-crobatics signaled her response: "As if."

The chick chat 'n' chew moved on. Alex tuned out. Which is when she heard, *I hope they don't see me.*

She grimaced. Another unasked-for break-in to Bree's brain? I'm grounded and I have detention, Alex thought. Isn't that punishment enough? She walked to the soda machine, but distance didn't drown out Brianna's monologue. *I can't do this. I won't. Oh, my god, how could she load me up with, like, eight thousand calories!* Alex was relieved when the bell rang, ending the lunch break.

"Bree?" Alex heard Cam say. "Hey," she whispered, "everything okay?"

Brianna chewed the inside of her cheek, then blinked rapidly. "Why wouldn't it be?" she responded, tapping her foot and looking everywhere except at Cam.

Oh, please, just go, Camryn. To Alex, Bree sounded more pitiful than impatient. She sounded whiny, Alex realized, almost as whiny as the woman in the snow.

"You waiting for someone?" Cam continued innocently.

"No," Bree snapped, then adjusted her tone. "I mean, Kris might meet me here. I'm just hanging for a minute. See you in language arts. Tootles."

Good! Bree breathed a sigh of relief when Cam walked away from her.

Alex started toward the door, determined to exit both the cafeteria and Bree's head. Only she couldn't do either one.

Go, Alexandra. Hello. What's she waiting for? I so do not need an audience.

That nailed it. The sullen desperation Alex had heard had been Bree's, not Miranda's.

Alex swung out the lunchroom doors, hoping to catch up with Cam. Her sister was nowhere in sight. She turned back to peer through the diamond-shaped window. Amid the stream of kids dropping off their trays and going off to class, Brianna did an abrupt U-ie. She strode quickly across the cafeteria to a trashcan at the far corner. There, Alex saw, she unzipped her backpack, took out her lunch bag, and dropped it into the rubbish.

Cam was already home and seemed to be engrossed in reading, when her sister finished her hour's detention and came in from the cold.

"Dude, the weirdest thing just happened —" Alex began.

"Give it a rest!" Cam held up her hand, which, Alex noticed, was trembling slightly. "Later," Cam added forcefully. "Right now, I'm totally maxed out on weird."

Alex shrugged, upended her backpack, and dumped its contents on the bed, aiming to deal with her own pile of homework. She opened her notebook but couldn't concentrate. Her mind kept wandering back to a place she so didn't want to be: the Land of Bree. What was the little princess angsting over? Why had she gone from Spandex to sweats? Where had she and Kristen actually been when they were supposed to be partying in L.A.? And, final question, why was Alex still privy to the blond sprite's panicky thoughts? It wasn't like Bree needed help the way she had at the bowling alley.

Fifteen minutes later, when Alex had finally gotten into remedial chem, Cam glanced at her watch, got up, and flipped on the small TV in their room.

"Yo, actual studying-in-progress here," Alex called to her.

"In case your hyper-hearing's on the fritz, it's the news," Cam shot back. "I have a current-events thing to do. But never mind, I'll be all sacrifice-girl to your sad little GPA and mute it." Which she did.

"Cami, what did Miranda look like? I mean, in your vision," Alex ventured.

"Actually, I didn't see her all that clearly," her sister answered, annoyed. "Small, blond — why?"

Before Alex spoke again, Cam shook her head, perplexed.

"Blond?" Alex asked.

"I know," Cam said, only now realizing that she, too, had thought it odd. "It's not the way I pictured her, either."

"What if it wasn't —" Alex began. But her words were drowned out by Cam's scream.

Alex leaped off her bed. "What? What happened?"

One of Cam's hands was clapped over her mouth, the other, still trembling, pointed at the TV.

There were snapshots of half a dozen people on the screen, under a network banner that read: "Hit-and-Run Rate Rises." Alex recognized one of the pictures. She jumped up, grabbed the remote, and hit VOLUME.

". . . eighteen-year-old Martha Perks of Sun Valley, whose dream of becoming an Olympic athlete was destroyed on a lonely Arizona highway, and the latest casualty, Elias McCracken of Carlston, California," the announcer was saying. ". . . He died earlier today from injuries suffered in the ninth hit-and-run fatality this month. Leaving a distraught wife and a one-year-old baby, McCracken was a freelance photographer —"

Before Alex could get the words out, Cam sputtered, "That's the guy!"

"Dude, he's the guy who took the picture of Thantos," Alex yelped.

"No, you don't understand!" Cam fell to her knees and covered her face with her hands. "He's the man I couldn't save."

CHAPTER TWELVE
ILEANA RETURNS

Ileana returned to the courtroom with a vengeance — heels clacking, cape flaring, her face contorted with determination. Heads turned as she marched down the center aisle of the dome to the People's bench.

Lady Rhianna shook her head in disbelief. "Back so soon?" she announced drolly. "You missed the best part. But I won't keep you in suspense. In a landslide decision, the Accused was found guilty of all charges."

"What a surprise," Ileana muttered.

Rhianna added, "With better timing, my dear, you could have skipped the entire trial."

Still standing, Ileana tossed back her golden hair. "Trial or travesty?" she rudely challenged. Karsh covered his face with his bony old hands, sensing that his audacious charge was just warming up.

"Did she say travesty?" Lord Grivveniss asked.

"I did, Lordship," Ileana answered, her voice rising so that all could hear her. "This entire procedure is a farce, a sham, a charade. Every witch and warlock in this sacred hall knows that the criminal who ought to be on trial today is Lord Thantos!"

The communal gasp practically emptied the dome of oxygen. A frantic buzz began, followed by spectators calling out their shock, disagreement, or approval. To his credit, Thantos barely blinked. He rose slowly from the Accused's table and, more slowly still, turned to gaze at the agitated crowd. As his dark eyes drifted over them, they fell silent one by one.

"Lord Karsh," he announced, sounding more amused than angry, "is this how you reared the child?" Utterly ignoring Ileana, he continued, this time addressing the trio of judges. "And is this, Exalted Elders, how the rude young witch is schooling my nieces?"

"Exalted Elders and members of the Unity Council," Ileana cried out, "I accuse Lord Thantos DuBaer of murder!"

"Silence!" Lady Rhianna shouted.

"He killed his brother Aron. Everyone knows it!" Ileana persisted. "New evidence suggests that he made off with Miranda while she was helpless, broken by misery, and incapable of good judgment. And that he knows where she is even now! This is the beast who pretends to care about their children!"

Lady Rhianna, her rich, brown skin turned ashen, stood and unfurled her great wings. The whooshing sound they made and the gust they unleashed silenced the crowd once more. "Enough, Ileana! Quiet . . . everyone." When her command had been fulfilled, she reeled in her wings and sat again. "Lord Thantos, Lord Karsh, approach," she ordered. Sassy as ever, Ileana followed Karsh — and, seeing this, Fredo, seeming nonplussed about the guilty verdict, strutted behind his brother. Rhianna glared at them.

"Oh, let them stay," Lady Fan said, her small dark eyes gleaming with excitement. "A trial like this comes along once in a century — and I'm too old to wait for another."

Lord Grivveniss chuckled.

"Fine," Rhianna gave in. "But do not speak" — this to Ileana and Fredo — "unless you're addressed directly, understood?"

"Understood," Ileana agreed. Fredo pretended to lock his lips with an imaginary key and toss it over his shoulder. "Esteemed trackers." Rhianna nodded at Thantos and Karsh. "This is a most unusual circumstance. Yet it presents a welcome opportunity. For both of you, it offers the chance to end the harsh rumors and suspicions that have brought discord to Coventry for fifteen long years.

"Lord Thantos, you've been very generous to us," Rhianna continued. "Your contributions helped to restore the great amphitheater. The computers you donated to the Unity Council have simplified our voting system. Can we not call upon you again — to clear your name and return true unity to our divided island? I urge you to think about it. And, Lord Karsh, will you represent our people once more by telling what you know and by asking aloud the questions that have been whispered about Lord Aron's death for more than a decade?"

"You dare ask me to stand trial for the death of my brother?" Thantos growled.

"Oh, is that what this is all about?" Fredo blurted. "No, no, no. You're barking up the wrong brother, Rhianna!"

"How would you know?" Ileana snapped at him.

"Silence," Rhianna shouted.

"He started it," Ileana protested.

With a cold smile, Thantos shook his head as if he were far above and weary of both of them. To Karsh, he said, "Have you any evidence linking me with the unfortunate incident?"

"Circumstantial at best," Karsh admitted.

"Circumstantial?" Ileana muttered under her breath. "Who came to call on Aron that very morning? Who was the last person Miranda saw him with?"

"You mean me?" Fredo asked. Thantos glared at him and Fredo again pantomimed locking his mouth and throwing away the key.

"Exalted Elders," Karsh addressed Grivveniss, Fan, and Rhianna. "As always, I will gladly do what you request of me. I will ask the questions. And then we may leave it to the Unity Council to vote —"

"With *his* computers!" Ileana balked.

"And I, also," Thantos offered, avoiding Ileana's blazing eyes, "will do whatever you think best."

And so it happened, the merely curious trial of Fredo DuBaer morphed into the most compelling one in all Coventry history. The Accused was the most revered and feared warlock of the island, the billionaire mogul, Lord Thantos DuBaer himself.

In accordance with the laws of the Unity Counsel, the Exalted Elders offered him a qualified advocate, as well as time to prepare a defense. The arrogant tracker refused both. "Help to clear my own name? I think not," he snarled. "Let's get this over and done with. It won't take long."

Karsh, too, waived time to present the People's case against Thantos. Had a day gone by in the past fifteen years when he hadn't thought about the devastating day or Aron's death? It was he — sadly, along with Ileana — who'd found Aron's bloodied body; who'd assumed the grim task of telling his wife and delivering Aron's bloody cloak to her. Miranda had told him precious little, but he would never forget her words: "Thantos came . . . but would not enter. Aron left to speak to his brother."

No, Karsh didn't need time to reconstruct what had most likely happened. It was a tale he didn't want to believe; a small part of him continued to balk. But he knew the story by heart. Aron left his wife and newborns, never to return.

The old man rose. On spindly legs, he made his way to the witness seat. His voice was rasping but steady. "I have known the DuBaer family for many decades. I watched the sons of Leila and Pantheas grow up — one with a brilliant mind, one canny but consumed with ambition, and" — Karsh looked down at his bony hands, avoiding Fredo's gaze. "One unfortunately slack-witted. Thantos, the eldest, admired all that Aron possessed: his keen intelligence, his beloved and equally gifted wife, his powerful twin children — most of all, the company founded by his brother —"

"Admired or coveted," Ileana murmured loud enough for many to hear.

Karsh ignored her. "The corporation known then as CompuMage, now DuBaer Industries. Aron and Thantos disagreed about how the company should be run, how its resources should be used —"

Ileana shot Thantos a sidelong glance. His face was a stony mask, but his eyes blazed with anger.

Karsh continued, "This is what I know and one thing more: Thantos was the last to see Aron DuBaer alive."

Silence fell over the amphitheater as Karsh bowed slightly to the Exalted Elders and retreated to the People's bench.

Thantos chose not to question Karsh but rose slowly and deliberately surveyed the amphitheater. Wordlessly, the hulking tracker demanded the rapt attention of every member present.

"Lord Karsh is right." The proclamation, declared in Thantos's deep booming voice, rocked the amphitheater. Until the menacing warlock thundered, "Right, that is, in his use of the word *alive*." He paused for effect. "I will recount what happened that tragic day." Thantos leveled piercing eyes at Karsh. "For I was there. The old man was not."

Ileana's face flushed with anger, but Karsh stilled her with a touch.

Thantos would not sit in the witness chair but paced as he talked, his hobnail boots pounding the gleaming floor of the amphitheater. "I came to my brother's door, this is true. He invited me to meet my newborn nieces. I very much wanted to, but urgent company business had arisen. I did not want to intrude on my dear sister-in-law's bliss, so I asked my brother if he would talk to me outside. Aron agreed. When I told him of the crisis at our company, he demanded I leave immediately for the CompuMage compound. It was not until the next day that I heard about Aron's murder. I was shocked and saddened."

"When you found out," Rhianna quizzed him, "why not return to Coventry Island? Aron was your brother."

Ileana could contain herself no longer. "You hid for fifteen years! You're a coward!" she shouted.

Thantos's face hardened. To Lady Rhianna, he said, "I knew nothing of the circumstances surrounding his death; there was nothing I could have added to the investigation. After that" — he whirled, staring straight at Ileana and without emotion — "it was just too painful. My beloved brother dead. My cherished sister-in-law vanished. My nieces under the protection of an arrogant young guardian. In the end, I did what Aron would have wanted: I made CompuMage the unrivaled company it is today."

It had come down to this: Karsh's circumstantial yet compelling argument versus Thantos's word.

As was customary in Coventry Island disputes, Lady Rhianna called for character witnesses. The Accused would begin. "There are many I could call," Thantos bellowed confidently, "countless who could attest to my exemplary character, but there is one known the world over, whose word is impeccable. I call the warlock Bevin Staphylus."

Ileana was puzzled. Bevin? Who was that? One of Thantos's lackeys, a tool, a turncoat? Ileana shaded her eyes against the glare of the lights. She saw him rise, and her hand flew to her mouth; her gasp became a strangled scream. Tall, handsome, and Armani clad, the young man swiftly approached the witness chair. His head was bowed, but Ileana, as millions of others would, recognized his distinctive body and stride. Brice Stanley. Her Brice. How could that be?

Thantos's thundering laugh filled the domed room. "Or should I say, Brice Stanley, as my former ward is now known. One of the biggest movie stars in the world!"

His ward? Ileana felt dizzy, her throat dry. If not for Karsh's steadying grip on her shoulder, she might have fainted.

His real identity shocked her. His testimony set her reeling. If what Brice said was truly unrehearsed, the actor deserved a second Oscar! He sat in the witness chair, suntanned and cool, expounding on all Lord Thantos had done for this community, how his generosity had aided charitable causes globally. Throughout his testimony, Brice avoided Ileana's eyes. He ended by reminding the Exalted Elders that Thantos, though reclusive, was too well known in the outside world to allow himself to stand trial if he were not completely innocent.

As Brice walked back to his seat, Ileana rose, pinning him with a searing stare. Blinded by rage and betrayal, she didn't notice the slight slump to his shoulders and surely knew nothing of the sadness in his heart.

A second character witness was summoned — this one by Karsh. "The People call Shane Argos."

It was Thantos's turn to be unpleasantly surprised. The handsome young Coventry Island native testified that he grew up believing legends of the brilliant and powerful Lord Thantos. When Shane came of age, he made no secret of his allegiance to the leader of the DuBaer clan. Not long ago, he'd helped the powerful warlock attempt to return Apolla and Artemis to their birthplace.

Thantos sat grim-faced. He knew what this boy would say.

Candidly, straightforwardly, Shane explained. "Had this trial taken place several months ago, I would have corroborated all Bevin testified to. But in recent months, I have witnessed another side to Lord Thantos. I no longer believe him incapable of murder."

"Tell the assembled what you witnessed," Lady Rhianna instructed.

Shane recounted Thantos's orders to make contact with the twins through one of their best friends, Beth Fish. The task successfully fulfilled, Thantos then casually ordered the young warlock to "dispose" of the innocent girl.

Thantos banged his fist on the Accused's table. "I said dispense with her . . . not kill her."

"Perhaps I misinterpreted your will," Shane stared daggers at Thantos, "or perhaps I interpreted it all too well."

Ileana knew what would happen now. Both sides would continue to present character witnesses, one refuting the other. Both had already presented believable testimony. The scale was evenly balanced. Without an eyewitness? The verdict would be rendered in favor of the Accused. An outcome Ileana could not allow. Karsh read her mind. "There is nothing more we can do, child. We must accept . . ."

"No. We mustn't," she countered, standing tall. An idea flew into Ileana's mind, fluttering there like a hummingbird. *If they can do it, surely I can, too.*

"You are thinking of the twins again?" Karsh said.

"Who, besides the murderer, is the only one who would know for certain where and how Aron was killed . . . and who did it?" Ileana asked. "The victim himself," she replied to her own question.

"Lord Aron?" Karsh was alarmed. "But he's dead."

"Did you know," Ileana asked, slipping her cape back on and feeling in its pocket for her *Little Book of Spells,* "that using the herb marjoram instead of mugwort changes the results of the Transporter spell?" she asked coyly.

"Marjoram, marjoram . . ." Karsh thought about it. "The herb helps one accept big changes in one's life. And, of course, in early times, it was said to escort the dead in their travels to other — no, Ileana," he whispered sharply. "You cannot seriously be thinking of summoning Aron to testify against his brother."

"Oh, can't I?" Ileana laughed.

CHAPTER THIRTEEN
MOJO IN NO GO?

A jarring screech came from Alex's guitar. She dropped it on the floor and jumped up, snapping her fingers. "Cam! You know what just hit me?"

"That you can't, in fact, play guitar?"

Alex ignored the lame quip. Her sister had been in a guilty funk all evening, ever since seeing McCracken's picture on the news. "We didn't do the Transporter spell wrong."

Cam's brow was furrowed. "Once more, for the slow section?"

Alex set down her guitar and paced the room. "Our magick got ahead of us, that's all. It knew, if we didn't, where at least one of us had to be. Someone needed help. Desperately. And you were there. You saved the mother and child."

"So what are you saying? Our magick has a mind of its own?" Cam scoffed uneasily.

"That's exactly what I'm saying," Alex insisted, excited. "Think about it: Did I ask to break into the shallow mind of your most superficial friend? Rhetorical question alert. I didn't have a choice. That night at the bowling alley, Bree was crying out for help."

It was happening with increasing frequency: Alex's extraordinary mind-reading power turning on and tuning in without her say-so, even against her own free will! Witness the stealth break-in today on Bree's bizarre thoughts. She had no clue what that was about.

Cam challenged, "If our magick is so smart, why did I manage to save only two out of three? I couldn't help the photographer."

Alex didn't want to say it. *Because you were up against a black belt tracker.*

"So in a battle of me against Thantos, he wins. I can't cut it?" Cam said glumly, replaying the events of yesterday in her head.

"Hit the escape key on the I'm-not-worthy screen," Alex advised. "Don't be so hard on yourself. Maybe you weren't a match for him alone, but together . . ."

"No!" Cam sprang off the window seat. She suddenly made a decision. Or maybe she was voicing one that had been brewing inside her since the hit-and-run.

"No, what?"

"You're mind-reader girl. Go for it. Wait, don't bother. If Uncle T wanted to scare me, guess what — score! I am handing in my resignation. I'm out of the witch business." Cam folded her arms.

Alex cracked up. "You're out of the witch business? As if you could be."

Cam walked up to Alex and looked into her twin's eyes. "Wrap your brain around this: Bad stuff is happening. We can't handle it. We need to summon Ileana. And Karsh."

"Busy signal," Alex reminded her. "Do not disturb. *Cerrado,*" she added in her best *Sesame Street* Spanish. Not wanting to be stunned, dazzled, poached, or roasted, she backed away to escape Cam's gaze.

"Thantos sent two of his thugs to kill McCracken and his family. This qualifies as 911!" Cam exclaimed.

"Your point? This isn't the first time he's offed someone. He murdered our father, Cam. And probably my late, unlamented adoptive dad, too." Alex bent over, picked up Cam's book, and chucked it on her sister's bed. "Anyway, this is our fight, not Ileana's."

Stubbornly, Cam said, "If you don't want to summon our guardians, fine. But I'm taking a pass. I'm off the case."

Alex refused to take her seriously. "Oh, just deal, Cam-ille. Our mom's alive. You sensed it. You 'saw' her. The notes prove you were right. All we have to do now is find her. And we aren't lead-devoid. We have two." She ticked them off. "One: wife of shutterbug. She's alive, thanks to you. She might know where Elias took the picture. And she owes you."

"What part of N-O don't you get?" Cam's patience was running out. The photographer's wife was on the West Coast. No way was she using the Transporter spell again.

Alex pretended she didn't hear Cam. "Two: Whoever's been sending the notes — even if it turns out to be our dear uncle Thantos — knows where she is. We find out who's doing it, we find our mother."

With or without Cami's help, Alex decided, she would get to the photographer's wife. For an encore, she would expose "anonymous."

Brianna Waxman was no part of this plan. Yet there she was, rattling around in Alex's brain again — tiny, tired, tart-tongued as ever. In school the next day, Alex found herself hyperaware of the elfin snob. Long on gossip, short on temper. Practically lost inside her economy-size threads. But brittle, as if she might snap in half at any moment. What was Bree's issue?

And what was Alex's? For instance, why, after lunch, was she sneaking around following Bree? This time, the brown bag went into the garbage in the girls' room.

"The Waxman heiress dumped her lunch," Alex told Cam later at her locker.

"And?" Cam scoffed, disinterested.

"This isn't the first time."

Cam rolled her eyes. "Hello, leftovers. Bree is hardly Ziploc girl."

"Okay," Alex said with a shrug. "You would know. She's *your* home girl."

"Anyway," Cam continued, annoyed that Alex thought she was an expert on friends Cam had known practically all her life. "She's always been weird about food. At PITS, she orders Beverly Hills pizza. Instead of cheese and sauce, it's topped with salad. Even then she cuts off the crust. Besides, if I know Bree, she probably called for a sushi takeout and had it delivered to her locker or something."

"In the category of 'If I know Bree' for the daily double, here's another puzzler," Alex challenged.

"Lay it on me." Cam feigned boredom.

"Remember that tasty tidbit Bree dropped the other day? Did she not say she was partying with Hollywood heartthrob Brice Stanley? Well, *Access Hollywood* states that Brice is on holiday, far from the movie crowd, in his retreat on an unnamed island."

"So, he's probably on Coventry. This relates to Brianna exactly how?"

"Timing," Alex responded. "How could he have been in L.A. on the chum-patrol with Bree at the same time?"

Cam sighed. "Brice Stanley is a warlock. Duh. Warlock. Transporter spell? Shape-shifting. He could totally be in two places — if not at exactly the same moment, he could commute from one to the other instantly, making it seem like that. Any of this sound familiar? As in . . . did we not just do something pretty similar?"

"That's your hypothesis," Alex said.

"And yours would be?"

"We know Kristen didn't go, and Brianna lied about that. I say Bree never went, either. Daddy dropped the ball again. Only this time, she was really too mortified to tell anyone."

Cam hadn't meant to stamp her foot. She almost took a header on the waxed linoleum. "I'm not 'anyone.' I'm one of her best friends. She would tell me."

Alex shrugged and walked away. Livid, Cam watched her go. If something were seriously wrong with someone as close to Cam as Bree was, her mojo would be in over-drive now. She would have had a premonition, a vision. She would just know.

"Sibling rift?" Cam held on to her locker handle this time as, startled, she spun to face Beth.

Pausing to make sure no one was in hearing range, Cam's tall, curly-haired bud followed up with, "Any progress on the mother search?"

What could Cam say? Thantos had Miranda locked away in some loony bin — and Cam couldn't get to her? "Not yet," she murmured, flipping the combination on her locker.

"You will," Beth said encouragingly. "BTW — did you remember to bring those bizarro notes?"

"Forgot." Cam flipped open the locker. Panic kicked in and she dropped her books. There was a note taped to the inside of the door.

"What is it?" Beth cried. "What's there?"

This one was a collage. Done in bits of material, cal-ligraphy, and strangest of all . . . letters pasted in bits of food.

Altogether, it spelled out: *Open your eyes, why can't you see what's happening to her? She's crying out for help — why can't you hear her?*

Cam couldn't stop trembling. Whoever left this note was mocking them — her supersight and Alex's keen hearing. She barely realized she was speaking aloud. "Whoever wrote this —"

Beth finished her sentence, "Is a copycat!"

"Huh?"

"This is totally Kristen's style," Beth pointed out. "You know that."

Cam stood there, dumbfounded.

"The calligraphy is just like the Chinese silk kind that Kris is learning," Beth explained. "And the food-as-art thing? Identical to the ones in her friendship collage."

"Someone's copying Kristen?" Cam repeated dumbly.

Beth arched her eyebrows. "Unless . . . it *is* Kristen."

Cam shook her head vigorously, as if she could shake off her rising panic. "Why would Kris be sending me anonymous messages about my mother? Make sense much?"

"Not even," Beth agreed.

CHAPTER FOURTEEN
STUDY BUDDIES

Brianna was clearly startled — and not in a good way — to find Cam's clone at her door. Not that Alex had expected a friendly welcome when she rang the bell.

Listening to Brianna thinking, *What's she doing here?* was unsurprising. Hearing her say aloud, "Love that Montana hat but trick or treat is months away. Lost much?" earned her honors in the totally rude category.

Alex deserved it, she guessed. Showing up on Bree's doorstep was kind of a stealth attack. Whether Cam agreed or not, Alex knew that the pint-sized girl was in trouble. Ignoring that fact, no matter how she personally felt about Bree, was not an option. Witching 101 demanded that she find out what was going on and help the girl. So Alex had talked Mrs. Olsen into giving her and Bree dual makeup tests. After balking, Bree had finally agreed to a study session. Only Alex neglected to mention that today after school was the only time she could do it.

At Bree's house.

Caught off guard, Bree went from rude to hostile. "No can do now. I'm on my way to the gym."

She didn't look it. She was still in the same clothes she'd worn to school — down to her Steve Madden slides.

Alex played the parent card. "Look, I'm grounded for the Tuesday cutting thing. This is the only way I could get out of jail free. Besides, we can do this in a half hour."

Bree wavered. *I don't want her to see my house! I told Cam not to bring her.* She had? Alex was stunned. Cam had never said a word about that. Not that Alex cared about Bree's crib, but what was up with that?

Whatever. Alex got back on track. "I borrowed Sukari's notes. If we start with them," she suggested, and went on and on about grade points and PSATs and college admission requirements until she finally wore Brianna down.

"Oh, fine. Come in. But a half hour, that's it." *Not that I care what she thinks, but . . . I'm sure she didn't expect this dump.*

Bree had that right. Casa de Waxman East was nothing like Alex expected. It wasn't even where she as-sumed it would be. The me-so-cool daughter of a him-so-hot Hollywood producer should have been living in swank Marble Bay Heights, in some palace fit for the princess she so was, right?

Nuh-uh. Turned out to be a modest suburban ranch in a modest suburban neighborhood. The biggest shock? Brianna's room. Expectations? Expensive, expansive, elaborate. Reality? Small, square, and spare.

"Mom's not home?" Alex asked, trying not to let her surprise show.

"She's at work," Bree replied.

"What does she do?" Alex had assumed the ex-Mrs. Waxman didn't work. All Brianna ever talked about was her dad and the mounds of moolah he had. Was this an-other Bree secret Cam purposely kept from her?

Brianna sighed. *Might as well tell her. It's not like I need to impress* her.

Thanks, Alex grunted.

"Four days a week, she works at a doctor's office. Two days, she works as a bookkeeper for an accountant. And on the seventh day, she cleans the house." Alex's eyes popped. Bree's mom worked two jobs — like Sara had? But that didn't make sense. For Sara Fielding it was about survival. Didn't Eric the great Waxman even sup-port his family?

Brianna snorted, "In case you're wondering, and I know you are, my dad would give us anything we want. He sends me money for clothes and stuff. But my mom won't take anything. She considers herself very proud. And independent." *And stupid,* Brianna added silently.

Alex could not believe she actually had something in common with Queen Bree. But she said, "My mom was the same way. Proud. And independent. She was a great role model."

"Lucky you," Bree said sarcastically. Then she sighed. "Look, you want a snack? I can probably dig up something."

While Bree was gone, Alex surveyed the room. Posters, magazine tear-outs, photographs — some of Brianna and the Six Pack, Bree and various boyfriends, but most of the snaps were family shots. Little Bree with both parents; with her dad and grandparents; preteen with her dad and some random starlet. Bree's dad young, with his arm around Redford and Newman; Bree's dad older, shaking hands with young movie stars; with politicians, holding up a poster and pointing to the line on it that said, *Eric Waxman Presents.* The room was like a shrine — to a dad she hardly ever saw.

When Bree returned with a bag of chips, a jar of salsa, and two bottles of water, Alex pointed to one of the framed photos. "How old were you when this was taken?"

"Around six or so, during my chubola period," Bree answered sourly. "I don't know why I even keep that one up there."

"You don't look chubby," Alex scoffed. "You look like a normal kid."

Normal enough for my parents to have split like a minute after that shot was taken. "I've been on the pudge patrol for, like, ever," Brianna said dismissively.

Which reminded Alex what Bree had thought of herself that night at the bowling alley. "Stupid, fat, and ugly." But that expression — heinous as it was — was like the theme song for half the girls at Marble Bay High and beyond. It didn't mean anyone really believed it. Did they?

"Anyway," Bree continued, "let's get this studying thing over with. I really need to hit the gym."

Alex tilted her head. "Want to come over for dinner?" *I can't believe I just invited her. . . .*

"Uh . . . *no!*" Bree wrinkled her nose and shot her such an "are you insane?" look that Alex immediately regretted asking.

Studying with Brianna turned out to be okay. The girl had smarts and deftly memorized charts, elements, chem facts. Except for a father and the pile of cash everyone thought she had, Brianna Waxman was doing all right. She was the total opposite of stupid, fat, and ugly. But why did she always front — act as if being Eric Waxman's daughter was the only thing that mattered?

As if Bree had tapped into her brain, the bitty blonde mentioned offhandedly, "My dad asked me to spend the summer in L.A. with him. But I'm so not bathing-suit ready yet."

"You should go," Alex said encouragingly. "Even though you practically just got back." Then she heard Brianna's tortured thoughts. *Just got back, right. Back from my backyard. Cam knows Kristen stayed home. But if anyone finds out that my dad never sent the tickets, I'll be like . . . no one.*

For the first time since realizing she could read minds, Alex had to work at not saying something about what she'd just heard. How could Bree not see that Eric Waxman's neglect made *him* a deadbeat dad? Yet her self-esteem was totally tied to him. That was warped.

CHAPTER FIFTEEN
DESTINY'S TWINS

Cam deliberately avoided mentioning the most recent note to Alex. Even though her scarlet-haired twin acted like the new Six Pack expert, Kristen Hsu was Cam's friend. And Cam wanted to think over what she'd just learned. All three anonymous notes were in Kris's style. Obviously sent by someone who knew Cam's locker combination.

Of course, almost any decent witch or warlock could copy Kristen's art and open a flimsy hall locker.

Cam decided she'd spill all to Als eventually but for now she wouldn't think about the mystery in Alex's presence. She'd figure it out first, alone.

Luckily, barring her twin from a mind break-in

turned out to be a cinch. Emily and Dave had impulsively gone straight from work to some cultural do in Boston. Hence, the kids were free from compulsory family time around the table.

Cam made herself a salad and tuna on toast and took it to her room. She could eat, mull over the notes, and finish her book report. No way would her sister, minus parental supervision, hang in the bedroom.

She had that right. Alex and Dylan gorged on junk food — frozen pizza, cheese sticks, microwave popcorn, Skittles, and soda — which they'd taken into the family room. There, blasting the TV and jamming on guitars, the two were in Friday night pig heaven.

Alex deliberately did not tell Cam about her field trip to Bree's. Why should she? All this time, Cam had made this big play of wanting Alex involved with her friends. But that clearly stopped short of full disclosure between them on "sensitive" Six Pack issues.

Cam had obeyed instructions to keep Alex away from Bree's place. So that meant, in a choice between her true-blue buds and a newfound sister, blood came in second. Alex shouldn't have been surprised, she told herself, or hurt. And if she'd learned a few things on her own, there wasn't any hurry to share them with a two-timing twin.

Avoiding each other was what they both wanted. So when the family phone rang and Cam grabbed it first, she didn't bother asking who was calling. She pushed down the feeling that the voice on the other end was vaguely, unsettlingly familiar, and hollered downstairs, "Alex, it's for you. Someone returning your call."

As soon as her twin picked up, Cam set down the receiver. Probably one of Alex's Montana homies, she tried to convince herself, even as her gut told her it was not.

Alex took the call in the kitchen, away from Dylan's ears.

The caller was Molly McCracken, the photographer's widow. After some intense Internet detective work — way to be a tracker, Alex thought proudly — she'd found Mrs. McCracken on her own. There were definite advantages to going to a school with an excellent computer lab. As she'd figured, the photographer's wife and her child were temporarily housed in a shelter in Carlston, California.

Before heading over to Bree's house, Alex had dialed the shelter's 800 number and left a message for Molly to call her back.

The moment Cam hung up the phone, Alex explained to the jumpy Molly that she was related to the girl who'd saved her life.

"What do you want?" Molly asked suspiciously. Alex

rushed to assure her that the only thing she wanted was the name and location of the sanitarium where the picture had been snapped.

There was silence on the other end. Alex held her breath. But when Molly finally spoke, it was only to say, "I wish I could help you. I don't know anything about the picture. I only know that Elias was in California when he took it. But I don't know where. And now it's gotten him killed . . ."

A few hours later, in the still of the night, Alex bolted up in bed. Something was wrong. She glanced over at her sister's bed. Cam was upright and staring at her.

"What is it?" Alex whispered. "How long have you been up?"

"I didn't tell you. I should have." Cam's voice was hesitant.

That's why she woke up, Alex thought. Cam's conscience was bothering her. Well, that was another thing they had in common — so was hers. Relieved, Alex cut in, "There's something I didn't tell you, either. About Bree —"

"I got another note," Cam said at the same time.

"One more thing," Cam interrupted. "I know who's been sending them. I just don't know why —"

CHAPTER SIXTEEN
I'LL NEVER TELL

Sneaking out of the house in the dead of night required stealth and absolute silence. Cam and Alex were on it.

It was after midnight when they layered up in jeans, matching dark turtlenecks, and multiple sweatshirts under jackets — Cam in her pink ski parka, Alex in an old quilted camo jacket.

Brushing by the full-length mirror, Cam couldn't help cracking, "Aren't we the fashionistas? We look like the Riding Hoods: Little Pink and Little Punk."

They tiptoed downstairs, slipped into their shoes — combat boots for Alex, Timberlands for Cam — and headed over to Kristen Hsu's house.

The big puzzler? What was Kristen's connection to their missing mom? How would she know their mother was dying?

Alex tightened her sweatshirt hood against the icy wind and finally said out loud what they'd both been thinking, "Unless she's Thantos's latest stooge?"

Their villainous uncle had tried to snare them before, by sending a messenger disguised as a friend. But he'd never used someone in Cam's closest circle.

Break one: Kristen's house was within walking distance.

Break two: Cam's excellence-driven friend had recently moved her bedroom to the basement, where she'd have more space and privacy and could stay up studying late into the night.

Break three: The basement window was accessible from the back of the house.

Alex kept a lookout while Cam knelt in the snow, peering in. As icy slush seeped through her jeans, Cam whined, "Just once, how about you try the sight thing?"

"Mute the moaning, just tell me what you see," Alex whispered impatiently.

The window was covered by mini-blinds. Cam focused, telescoping in on the big dark room, and saw Kris, asleep, clutching a ragged old teddy bear. Alex raised her hand to rap on Kris's window. "You'll scare her. She'll scream," Cam cautioned.

"Better idea?" Alex challenged.

"Um . . . wiggle the teddy bear to wake her?"

Staring into the dark room, Alex imagined the plush toy rocking back and forth . . . saw its stiff little stuffed arm poking Kristen gently in the face . . . on the nose, she thought, amusing herself. One little stuffed sausage of an arm batting Kris's nose. *Pow!*

"Very funny," Cam scolded as Kristen's eyes flew open and she cautiously touched her nose. Cam tapped on the glass and called out quickly, "Kris! It's Cam! Don't scream! Come to the window!"

The slender girl was up instantly. And out the door almost as quickly. "What is it? Why are you here? Did something happen?" Kristen was quaking. She'd thrown a robe over her pajamas, but no coat. Her questions were a run-on sentence, punctuated by chattering teeth.

"Kris, I'm sorry we had to do this —" Cam began.

Alex cut to the chase. "Why are you sending us anonymous notes?"

"If you are," Cam backpedaled, but Kris's reaction told her it was true.

Alex could hear the girl's heart quicken and listened in to her thoughts: *Finally! They figured it out! Please don't let it be too late!*

Kristen didn't say anything out loud, just rubbed her arms in an attempt to warm up. "Maybe we should go inside," Cam suggested.

She shook her head, her long, lustrous hair looking enviably unruffled by sleep. "I can't. We'll wake them."

"Then let's make this quick." Alex so wished she could say, I know what you're thinking. All she did say was, "Spill."

The girl was shaking. Cam slipped off her ski jacket and put it around Kris. Head bent, eyes downcast, Kris admitted quietly, "I only meant to send one."

It was the answer they expected. Still, Cam was shocked. "But you don't know anything about her. How could you be sending those messages?"

Kristen's head snapped up. "Who would know her better than I would?"

Alex tuned in to Kris's panicked brain. *If they can't save her, I . . . I don't know what to do. She could die.*

"Who put you up to this?" Alex demanded.

Cam gripped Kris by her shoulders and implored her, "Someone is playing a trick on you, Kris. We know you're the messenger. Just tell us where she is and how to find her."

"Don't worry about Thantos," Alex added.

"Are you guys insane? She's at home. Where else would she be?" Frustrated and shivering, Kristen cried out, "And what's a Thantos?"

"This is our mother we're talking about!" Cam blurted, louder than she'd intended. "Stop pretending you don't know."

"Our birth mother, Miranda, could be dying — and you know it." You just thought that, Alex wanted to shout. She managed, "Or you wouldn't be sending us those warnings."

"Huh?" Kristen stared at Cam, then at Alex.

Alex heard the girl's heart flutter. She repeated, "Why are you sending us notes about our mother? Who put you up to this?"

And then little Kristen exploded. A volcano of pent-up emotions erupted. She put her fists on her slender hips and, in a voice way too big for such a small-boned girl, shouted, "Your *mother*?! Why would you think for a minute the notes were about your mother? Can you *really* be that self-absorbed?!"

Cam and Alex were shocked into silence.

"Well, of course they are. I mean, if not her . . . then . . . who?" Cam sputtered, wounded.

Confused, Alex asked, "Who are the notes about, then? And why send them to us? Who's dying?"

Kristen shook her head and sobbed. "I can't tell you. I promised. If you guys can't figure it out . . . I can't tell."

Alex got it. "A secret." She whispered, "Like in your collage. You made a vow to keep a secret. And now you're choking on it."

Whose secret would Kris be keeping . . . ? Before Cam finished the question, she knew the answer.

Brianna!

My vision, Cam telepathically reminded her sister.

Small, blond, Alex remembered. And the voice that had been frightened, but whiny, brittle. *It wasn't our mom. It was Bree!* Cam told her. *It all fits. Bree was in the snow because she was here, not in L.A.*

And postscript, Cam thought, *it happened practically the moment Snibble said, "Does anyone know where Brianna is?"*

Alex's shoulders slumped. She felt horrible — not only for Kristen and Brianna, but for herself and Cam, too. Of course it all fit. Hadn't she just found out that Bree never went to L.A.? That the girl had self-esteem issues to the max. She — and Cam — had seen and heard only what they'd wanted to instead of what was right in front of them.

Which was worse? Being blind to a friend in need

or taking three giant steps backward in the quest to find their mother? Cam didn't know. She inhaled the cold air. It stung her throat. *Ileana knew the messages weren't about our mother.*

Kristen noticed the silence but not the silent exchange. Cam put her arm around the sobbing girl. "What's wrong with Brianna?"

"I couldn't tell. I tried to show you instead."

"Why'd you pick us?" Alex pretty much knew the answer.

Kristen wiped her eyes on the sleeve of Cam's jacket and snuffled, "Because I thought you guys could help. Ever since you got here, Cam's mojo has gone over the top. I thought this would be easy for you. I never imagined you'd be so involved in your own drama, you'd totally be blind to a friend's — at least not you, Cam."

Cam winced. Alex grumbled, "Thanks."

"Just open your eyes!" Kristen implored them. "Bree can't even see what's happening to her. How come I'm the only one who can? When I tried to talk to her about it, she just shut down and made me swear not to mention it again, to anyone. But I'm her best friend. I can't just let it happen."

The puzzle pieces suddenly and sharply rearranged

themselves. The big clothes that hid Bree's shrinking body, her sallow complexion, the nonstop exercising, stealth lunch dumps, lying, and secrecy. It was suddenly so obvious.

Brianna Waxman was starving herself to death.

CHAPTER SEVENTEEN
THE CAVES OF COVENTRY

There were many places spirits gathered. The ancient oak in Mariner's Park was one; the one, Ileana remembered, where Karsh's great-great-great-grandmother — a healer — had been hanged for practicing witchcraft during the dark days of Salem. The sacred stream that fed Crow Creek was another. And it was there that the twins claimed to have met their grandmother — the late matriarch of the DuBaer family: Leila, mother of Aron, Thantos, and Fredo.

There was another, Ileana suspected. She unfurled her cape and returned to the dark side of Coventry Island, where Crailmore, the DuBaer fortress, stood. The caves of Coventry tunneled directly under the great stone fortress, where generations of DuBaer witches and warlocks had lived and died. It was there Aron's spirit was most likely to rest — if it could rest, knowing the perils his children faced at the hands of his murdering brother.

Ileana hurried through the forest, then fought her way through the dense bramble that hid many of the cave entrances. By the time she found the mouth of the largest cavern, her magnificent robe had been snagged on thorns and thistles, and a crown of vines, tree bark, and dead leaves wound through her golden hair. Nevertheless, she had succeeded. Her heart quickened by victory and expectation, she knelt at the entrance to the sacred cave and assembled her tools.

Marjoram and mugwort, Ileana had brought both. Candles made of beeswax; opal, stone of the spirits, and sapphire to help find lost truths; agate geode and quartz crystal both, to concentrate and enhance her psychic powers. Touching her head to the frost-powdered ground, cleansing her hands in the snow, Ileana inscribed a circle around her and, within it, set up her candles and stones and sprinkled both marjoram and mugwort.

Then she recited the Transporter incantation.

A wave of dizziness hit her, forcing her to close her eyes. Immediately, she felt her body being lifted from the ground. A whirling wind coiled around her, droning deafeningly. She felt as though she were caught in a tornado or a cyclone but one that was oddly warm, and embracing.

Losing all sense of time — and of danger — Ileana allowed herself to be spun in space until, with an unexpected jolt, she was dropped onto a sharp, rocky surface where an icy draft blew.

Slowly opening her eyes, she saw that she was deep inside the cave. No earthly light hinted at an entrance or exit. Yet something bright radiated a few feet before her. A glow that grew brighter and windier and colder.

"At last, you come!" a deep, almost angry voice rang out. It was not Aron's voice, yet not unlike his.

"I come for Aron DuBaer," Ileana said with as much courtesy as she could muster. She didn't like being shouted at. Still, it was important to show respect to the spirits, even bellowing, ill-tempered ones. "Lord Aron, father of the twins Artemis and Apolla," she explained to the strange light.

As she watched, it changed shape, took shape, transformed, as though through generations, from one murky being into another and another. Hopeful that the light's journey would end as Aron, Ileana knelt on the floor of the cave and waited as patiently as was possible for her under the circumstances.

"You seek my son?" The smoky form before her took the shape of a woman.

Swallowing her disappointment, hoping the spirit wasn't really finished morphing, Ileana studied the tall, stiff-shouldered aristocrat who held a cane in one of her age-dappled, bejeweled hands.

Then she realized what the woman had said. "Your son?" Ileana asked.

"Lord Aron DuBaer, father of Artemis and Apolla, husband of the widowed Miranda," the old lady said in her booming, none-too-friendly voice.

"Then you must be —"

"Your grandmother Leila!"

Ileana shook her head. "You mean, grandmother of the twins, right?" *Oh, no.* The young witch trembled in honest terror. *She's going to tell me that Fredo is my father.*

"That dolt!" the spirit Leila said. "My own son, and yet he is incapable of fathering anything but those thick-headed boys; vengeful, wanton dimwits!"

"Vey and Tsuris?" Ileana asked, unimaginably relieved.

The old woman waved her hand dismissively. "Tell me, why do you seek the spirit of my cherished son?"

Did Leila know that Aron had been murdered, Ileana wondered suddenly. Maybe spirits were spared the heartbreak of knowing how their children died. Ileana didn't know and didn't want to be the one to break such news — even if the "news" was fifteen years old.

"Well, well, how thoughtful of you." Leila laughed. "So there is a kind bone in your body —"

Ileana bristled. "I haven't much time, your Lady-ship —"

"Call me goddess," Leila snapped.

Ileana was momentarily taken aback. Then she quickly returned to her mission. "Goddess," she said, "I seek your son to ask him how he was killed. And by whom," she added softly.

"Child, let me look at you, for who knows when I shall see you again? I am your grandmother. Truly."

Ileana felt her chin being raised, although the woman before her had not lifted a hand.

"And as ashamed as I am of how your father hurt you," Leila continued, peering at Ileana with gray eyes, as metallic and gray as the twins' remarkable eyes and Ileana's own. "Still more am I ashamed of how I hurt him. My dear Ileana, little goddess — which I called you at your birth — if not for my stubbornness and arrogance, you might never have been cast out. But then, the mighty tracker Karsh would not have reared you. And, truly, he has given you all that your prideful family could not. It turned out for the best. Yet, for my part, I am sorry."

Ileana heard the droning start up again in her ears. Her head was addled with information and emotions. She wanted to ask the question Karsh had never answered for her — who is my father? Was there another brother no one spoke of who'd sired her? She wanted to be able to talk with Aron, to have him say that, yes, Thantos had murdered him. She would beg his spirit to appear at the dome. She wanted to know exactly what Leila was apologizing for. But the noise, the droning that grew louder by the moment, told her that the wind would whisk her back soon.

"Grandmother," Ileana called out in desperation.

The single word, like a powerful incantation, quieted the dizzying noise, but only for a moment. Slowly, the whooshing babble and the cave's cold breath began to well up again.

"Quickly, little goddess mine, choose your question, for each moment that I am in your world, the strength that I brought with me fades." Leila's voice had grown soft. The wind in the cave seemed to blow each word away from Ileana's ears.

She had too many questions. Which one mattered? Which one, she was startled to find herself wondering, should be asked for the good of Coventry Island? The good of the people? Never, in all her years, had Ileana ever considered or cared about such an outcome. Never had she placed the good of others above her own vain interests.

The fading light before her, the light that was spirit, seemed to glow inside her, to warm and "lighten" her. Ileana began to laugh.

"The question, the question!" Leila's vanishing voice urged.

The trial, Ileana thought, still smiling, still feeling lighthearted. The trial was important. The twins, equally important. The truth most important of all. The community must know the truth about what happened the morning Artemis and Apolla were born. "Was Aron murdered by his brother?" Ileana asked.

"Yes," Leila answered.

Ileana knelt. "There is little time, I know. But I beg you. Can you travel with me and reveal that truth to one and all?"

"This is what you wish? You would have me enter the sacred dome?"

"More than anything."

Leila held Ileana's eyes a moment more. "My child, little goddess," she cautioned, "be careful what you wish for."

CHAPTER EIGHTEEN
BRIANNA'S BREAKDOWN

They did not call in advance. Answering the door without makeup, Brianna looked frighteningly drawn, her face haggard and blemished. Even her hair seemed to be thinning.

"OMG, one wasn't enough," she cracked tiredly. "You're into serial ambushing now?" She glanced past them and saw, at the curb, smoke curling from the tailpipe of Dave's waiting car. "Wow, it's a family affair."

"Get dressed," Cam said gently. "Let's talk."

Bree looked at them, cocking her head, trying to act like her old cheerfully untroubled self. "Which one of you is going to read me my rights?" It didn't work. Finally, she sighed. "Okay, officers. I'll be right back."

"Dress warm," Alex called after her. "We're going to Mariner's Park. Cam's idea," she added.

Bree glanced at Alex over her shoulder. "I don't think so," she said, then disappeared toward the bedroom.

"My idea?" Cam grumbled.

"To be someplace magical where witches have a history," Alex reminded her. And, though it probably wasn't the best time to challenge her clique-centric sister, she couldn't help mentioning, "I heard through the mind-vine that Bree's crib was off-limits to me. Thanks for the heads-up."

Busted. "That was a tough one," Cam conceded. "It's just so important to her that everyone thinks she's this pampered rich babe. We know the truth, but we're her friends. . . . We keep her secrets. Don't say it —" Cam warned.

Even if keeping those secrets is dangerous and destructive? Alex didn't say it. But she thought it, loudly.

"Besides," Cam went on the defensive, "it's not like you ever asked to go there. There's a lot you didn't want to know about Bree. It was easier for you to hang on to your prejudice. You made it easy for me to do what Bree wanted."

"Now we've got to do what she doesn't want," Alex said.

"Thanks for the irresistible invite," Brianna said, returning to the front hall in sweats and sneakers. "But, you know, now that I've really thought about it? I'm gonna take a Pasadena on the field trip and hit the gym instead."

"Wait." Cam was calm but determined. "There's a reason we're asking you. It's not some random field trip."

"Oh?" Brianna arched her eyebrows. "Buried treasure hunt? Scavenger hunt? Cute-boy enclave? Somehow, I think not."

"We have something for you," Alex said, sticking with the plan. "And in a way, it is sort of like buried treasure."

Bree shot a sharp glance at Cam.

"We do have something to give you. It's kind of precious, too." It felt as though Cam were seeing her sick friend for the first time. Her voice was thick with emotion.

And maybe that's what did it. Brianna grimaced, glanced over Cam's shoulder, waved at David Barnes waiting in the car, and caved. "Okay, I'll play. How long will it take to bestow your gift? There's not a treadmill or bike left at Gym World if you get there late."

Cam's dad dropped them off at the entrance to Mariner's Park. The paths were already peopled by morning joggers and dog walkers, puffing smoky breath.

"Got your cell phone?" Dave asked Cam. Alex, and even Bree, cracked up. "I withdraw the question — on the grounds of 'way obvious,'" he admitted. "Call if there's any problem. Promise?"

As the trio traipsed up the hill leading to Cam's special place, Bree whined, "This better be extraordinary. Exemplary. Outstanding. In other words, twin-pains, this little excursion had better be worth it."

Or what? Alex was tempted to say.

Cam kicked her sister's ankle. "Promise. You will so thank us for this."

Eventually, Alex thought and swung her foot away to avoid another boot nudge.

Cam had brought a blanket and set it out under the gnarled oak tree. Alex had brought the crystals.

Brianna grudgingly sat between Cam and Alex and held out her palm. "Deliver. What's the gift? And why hide it here?"

Although she'd rehearsed it, Cam didn't know if she could say it, now that she was face-to-face with her friend. How long had this been going on? Cam's stomach turned as she noticed bony knees, pointy shoulder blades jutting from Bree's sweatshirt. There was a lump in her throat, but she got it out. "The truth is a gift, Brianna."

"Yeah, if you can't afford diamonds." Bree rolled her once-vibrant green eyes and started to get up. "Look, whatever new enlightenment you guys are into? Don't drag me all Dalai Lama with you. Just count me . . . out. I can't believe I let you talk me into this."

Alex held Bree's arm and said firmly, "It's okay. We know."

"What is it you think you know?" Bree challenged.

Cam blurted, "You're starving yourself. You have an eating disorder. You need help."

Bree's reaction was a shocker. She burst out laughing. "I wish."

"No!" Cam had to work to keep calm. "I mean, no one would wish that."

Bree wrapped her arms around her knees, a look of disgust clouding her face. "Starving? As if. I'm blubber! I could live off my fat."

"Oh, man, that is so warped!" Alex exclaimed.

Bree snickered, "This is what you dragged me here for? I am so gone. I'm calling a cab. She whipped out her cell phone and started to stand up.

"You can't go, you can't run away." Cam knew she sounded desperate. "Not until you realize what you're doing to yourself. And let us help you."

Brianna had ceased to be amused. She was getting angry. "Ready, aim, misfire. I neither want nor need your misguided help, Goody Four-shoes. You can't force me to stay here and listen to this bogus junk."

The twins looked at each other and shrugged. Cam

reached inside her sweatshirt and pulled out her sun charm, which glinted in the early daylight.

Alex did the same with her moon charm, rubbing it between her thumb and forefinger.

"What is this, a QVC moment? Selling your jewelry? Do I look like I need to accessorize?" Brianna was nervous as Cam locked eyes with her.

The Truth Inducer. It was one of the first incantations they'd learned. It had to work.

If it didn't, Cam thought, repulsed at the prospect, Brianna, whose first priority had always been "looking good," could soon be hospitalized against her will. Then everyone would know. How devastating would that be for someone who needed to keep up appearances?

If she had some control over things, like if she decided to get help voluntarily, Bree could spin the situation to her advantage. But to control it, she needed to accept it.

Cam grasped one of Brianna's bony hands, Alex the other. Bree pulled away. "What are you doing now? Contacting the dead?"

Just at that second, a warm breeze blew by — strange for the cold morning. It prickled the nape of Cam's neck, producing goose bumps. Alex felt it, too. And caught the clean, herbal scent of their guardian. "Ileana?" she whispered.

Or Leila, Cam guessed, remembering the regal spirit of their grandmother who had appeared to them once before.

Bree's tugging snapped them back to reality. She wasn't strong enough to slip out of their grip. "How can you do this to me?" she demanded as Alex and Cam began reciting the incantation. "You kidnapped me and now you're doing — I don't know what, but I don't like it. You're supposed to be my friends!"

"O sun that gives us light and cheer, shine through us now to banish fear . . ."

At once, Cam and Alex felt their amulets begin to heat and vibrate between their fingers. And then, as had happened before, the necklaces pulled toward each other as if magnetized, drawing Cam and Alex together. Clinging to Brianna's hands, the girls now formed a circle as tight and complete as their sun and moon charms did when they linked.

Brianna's green eyes glazed over. She stopped resisting the twins — her angry jaw relaxed. The charms separated, allowing the twins to sit back.

To Cam's gentle query, the gaunt girl confessed that she liked dieting. The more weight she lost, the prettier she felt. "One day, I'll look like the actresses my dad sees. Then he'll see me."

Cam's eyes welled with tears. Brianna felt invisible

to her dad — duh! Only now, Cam thought, Bree was making herself invisible for real. It didn't make sense.

Is it her way of getting back at him? she silently ventured to Alex.

Alex shrugged. *Maybe her way of having some control over her messed-up family. Isn't she all about control?*

Irony alert: Bree had no control over what she was doing to herself. And no clue about how she really looked. Kristen had been right.

Cam tried again. "This isn't the way. You're only hurting yourself, Bree — and everybody who loves you. All your friends, your mom and your dad." She added, "I'm sure," though she wasn't sure at all about Eric Waxman.

She was unprepared for Bree's outburst, Bree's truth: "You don't understand! When I'm thinner, he'll pay attention to me. He hates me because I'm so fat and ugly now."

Frustrated, Cam turned to Alex. "She still doesn't see it!"

"Then show her," her twin suggested.

Cam caught her breath. Instantly, she knew what Alex meant — which didn't make it doable. "But how? I've never tried that before — shared a vision, showed it to someone else."

"Maybe it was never this important before," Alex said.

Brianna was on ice, literally. The Truth Inducer had left her limp and perplexed for the moment. She sat quietly waiting now.

Cam closed her eyes and tried to recall her vision of the terrified girl in the snow, so thin, almost transparent. *Let this work,* she begged silently.

Concentrate, Alex urged, seemingly from far away. And then, as the vision returned in vivid detail, down to the bare trees, the snow, the brick house — which Cam now realized was Bree's home — and the girl begging for someone to understand her, Alex said excitedly, "That's it. You're doing it. I can hear it perfectly . . . and, Cami, I feel it, feel it out there, the coldness, the despair —"

Big glitch: Cam re-created the vision, Alex felt it, but Bree was the one who needed to see it.

Cam urged suddenly, *Use your mind, Alex. Move the sounds, the feelings, the whole vision if you can. Move it from us to Bree. Let her see what she looks like through other people's eyes.*

I don't know how, Alex confessed. *I don't know if I can move something . . . intangible . . . a thought, an image — from your mind to Bree's.*

The moment she told the truth, she was able to picture the vision as Cam described it. She imagined herself holding on to it, as if it were a painting or a drawing and not a moving image. And then she pictured folding the paper on which she'd transferred the vision. Folding it into a paper airplane that she struggled to grasp and sail toward Bree.

"Oh!" the subdued, skeletal girl exclaimed, moving suddenly. "Ouch, what's that?" She ruffled her hair, rummaged through it as if she were searching for something. And then her eyes widened as whatever she'd been looking for seemed to unfold inside her head.

A horrified scream snapped Cam and Alex out of their deep concentration. It was followed by, "Oh, my God, that's me. Oh, no. Is that what I look like?"

Brianna covered her face and wept. Cam — and Alex, for a while — wept with her.

Over the next few days, Brianna took her first steps toward getting well. It meant getting help — quickly — the kind that could only come from parents.

Brianna's mom was shocked and so very ashamed she hadn't seen it. She'd been so busy, working to stay independent, she had really thought her daughter was doing well. Mrs. Waxman came down hard on herself.

Emily stepped up to the emotional plate, assuring Bree's mom that it wasn't at all unusual for a parent not to realize what was happening. "If your daughter wants to hide something from you" — she paused to wink at Cam and Alex — "there's not much you can do. They know exactly how." She quoted studies showing that even the most attentive parents don't always notice. And that the important thing was getting Brianna help. Cam was proud of her mom. Alex was proud of her legal guardian.

Then Dave stepped up to the practical plate. Calling in one of the doctors his firm had worked with in the past, they double-teamed Eric Waxman until he understood just how serious, how dangerous his daughter's condition was and exacted a promise that the neglectful Hollywood mogul would shell out whatever it took for Brianna's well-being.

Shame, guilt, and the possibility that his child would land on the cover of *People* as the latest Hollywood eating disorder casualty soon had Bree's dad securing a bed for her at a highly regarded rehab. The place was secluded, tucked away, expensive, and very private. And, after checking the stats, Dave announced that its success rate was top-notch.

Neither he nor Brianna's dad would divulge the clinic's name right now — at least not until Brianna's recovery was well under way.

"Nothing but the best for my best girl," Alex and Cam overheard Mr. Waxman bragging.

"Bree's condition must be contagious," Cam said, disgustedly. "'Cause I just so lost my appetite."

CHAPTER NINETEEN
SAYING GOOD-BYE

Saying good-bye to their friend was the hardest thing the Six Pack, as a group, ever had to do. But on a weekday afternoon at the end of March, they gathered to support her, reassure her, help her . . . and show her they loved her.

They made her a card and a gift basket. Kristen put in the teddy bear she slept with, so Brianna might feel more secure. Amanda made her a power bracelet, "for health and inner strength." Beth gave Bree a journal; Sukari a good luck stone with the word BELIEVE carved into it. Cam had inserted a Discman into the basket, and Alex had burned a CD with meaningful songs. Mostly, they gave her hugs.

They promised, one by one, that e-mails would be flying and phone bills would mount. They'd be in touch every single day.

Later, at Pie in the Sky, the Six Pack, minus one, sat in their usual booth and, over pizza, tried to understand. How could their closest friend have an eating disorder — and they not know it? Were they all self-absorbed? Or was Bree just that good at hiding her problem?

Why hadn't anyone realized the girl's obsessive dieting had gotten out of hand, and she'd become an anorexic? No one except Kristen had figured it out, and she'd been sworn to secrecy. A secret she'd nearly choked on, so as not to "betray" a friend.

The definition of friendship was now something they were all choking on. Wouldn't Kris have been a better friend if she'd just told someone, an adult?

Sukari insisted that's what she would have done. "If it's something that serious, where's the decision? You do what's best for the person, even against her will. That's what makes a friend."

Beth reminded Suke that unless she'd really been in Kris's shoes, she couldn't really know what she would have done. Then the curly-haired girl put her arm around Kristen. "You made a choice. You did what you could. I think you're an incredible friend."

The tears around the table flowed so freely that Dylan, at the next booth with his friends, jokingly sent a pail and mop over.

Alex was relieved that Brianna was getting help, but she couldn't stop thinking that Bree's good fortune was their rotten luck. The notes had not been about Miranda. So, as far as finding their mother was concerned, they were back where they started.

Or were they?

"Are we even sure now that our mother is in an asylum?" Cam backpedaled.

"There's a reason Thantos wanted that picture destroyed, that he went ballistic when it was printed," she told Cam on the way home. "He so didn't want anyone to know where he was."

"And Fredo did say, 'She went mad. She had to be put away.'" Cam shuddered, remembering their uncle's callous words.

"So let's kick it up a notch," Alex suggested. "We have, like, this massive amount of research to do. Molly McCracken said the pic was snapped in California. Boot up the search engine and type in 'Loony Bins, CA.' We start."

Cam hesitated. "But what about Molly? Our uncle's probably the one who sent that car careening around the corner to mow down her husband. I keep feeling we should be able to help her."

Alex agreed, and then she realized how they could do just that.

Thankfully, David Barnes didn't ask too many questions. He just jumped in with two feet, becoming Mrs. McCracken's pro bono lawyer and getting Molly the money she was owed from *Starstruck,* "the big score" the magazine had tried to send her husband. Interns at Dave's law firm also helped, finding housing, child care, and even counseling for Elias's widow.

"You're the best, Dad!" Cam hugged her father hard when she found out what he'd done.

"Uh, yeah, what she said," Alex agreed shyly. She took a pass on the hug. This time.

CHAPTER TWENTY
SECRETS AND LIES

Ileana returned to the amphitheater feeling changed, different, and proud of herself. She had made a choice, the sort of choice she'd never really considered before. She'd chosen the welfare of others over her own selfish concerns and was about to see truth and justice rendered once and for all.

And she'd been given the chance to do it by her grandmother! Her own flesh and blood.

Ileana laughed at the expression. Leila was not exactly "flesh and blood." She was spirit, the spirit of a wise and beautiful woman who was Ileana's own grandmother. Amazing!

"What have I missed? What's happened?" Ileana

whispered to Karsh, after tiptoeing down the aisle and slipping back into her seat beside him.

"I might ask you the same thing," Karsh said, examining her glowing face, on which the hint of a smile still shone. "What's happened to you? You look positively . . . transformed."

Yes, do tell us all!

Lady Rhianna hadn't spoken the words aloud but fired them silently at Ileana and Karsh like a schoolmarm hurling an eraser. She then turned to the Accused's table — where Thantos sat glaring and Fredo, grinning — and slyly answered Ileana's question. "Lord Thantos has produced several more witnesses, all attesting to his sterling character. Lord Karsh has presented others, of opposite opinion. We are now ready to vote."

Fredo stood abruptly. "Order in the court. Order in the court," he demanded. "No one asked me anything! When do I get to tell my side of the story?"

"Sit down," his brother commanded. "You have no side!" And Fredo did.

"Wait." Ileana stepped forward. "If it pleases the court . . ."

"I'm sure it doesn't," Rhianna responded.

"I have another witness. Someone who knows the truth. Someone from whom the murderer could not hide." She narrowed her startling eyes at Thantos, who stared back, his jaw set.

Fredo started to whimper, but Thantos clapped his huge paw over his brother's face.

"Let her play this out. It should be very interesting," he said.

"Oh, it will be," Ileana retorted.

She bowed her head, and as Leila had instructed her, tossed a handful of mugwort and marjoram into the center of the amphitheater. She chanted, "I call on the spirit of a mother proud and unbowed, she who dwells in a world beyond. I call on the one who knows the truth and no fear. I call the spirit of Leila DuBaer!"

A blinding light filled the room, and then, though no windows were open, a gust of swirling wind formed, tornadolike, directly in front of the trio of the Exalted Elders. Ladies Rhianna and Fan and Lord Grivveniss were shocked into silence, along with everyone in the room. They watched in awe as the swirling took shape, silhouetted now in an unearthly glow. In seconds, the regal spirit of Leila DuBaer appeared.

Thantos's rage got stuck in this throat. He started. "This is a hoax. She cannot . . . !" For once, the mighty tracker could not finish his thought.

Lady Rhianna was awestruck. "How did . . . ?"

Grivenniss finished the sentence, ". . . she do that?"

Karsh was overcome with pride — and panic. He did not know the depth of Ileana's talents and perhaps never would. He feared for her.

"The spirits of our dead cannot rest," Ileana declared, ". . . not until justice is served. Even if the spirit must reveal a heinous family secret."

Karsh stood and bowed his head. "Lady Leila, we welcome you."

"You know I can't stay," the spirit whispered, lifting her head to gaze at the Elders.

Ileana charged forward. "I will be brief. Just a few moments ago you told me that your son Aron was murdered at the hand of his own brother."

"He was," Leila replied sadly.

"How do you know? Were you there?" Ileana gently asked.

"I didn't have to be there. I know my sons. The murderer confessed to me — he was so . . . proud! Of what he'd done."

"I ask you now, cherished spirit, is the murderer of your son Aron in this amphitheater?"

"He is." For a split second, Leila's regal bearing faltered. Her light began to soften, to fade.

Dizzy with dread and excitement, Ileana panicked.

No! She couldn't leave, not yet. She hurried on. "Can you point him out?"

The spirit turned slowly. An outstretched arm pointed straight to the table of the Accused. Ileana held her breath.

Leila's steely gaze fell on Thantos. "How could you?"

And then, slowly at first, but deliberately, like a Ouija board's pointer, she turned, her accusing finger moved past Thantos. It stopped when it landed on . . . Fredo. When Leila spoke, it was clear she was using the last of her earthly energy. "You were supposed to take care of him!" she cried to Thantos. "He was incapable of taking care of himself! You made a vow. Were you so enraged at my disapproval of your bride that you exacted revenge by betraying me? By breaking your promise? How else to explain why you allowed Fredo to kill my beloved Aron?"

The reaction to Leila's stunning revelation was profound and protracted. There was not a soul in the Coventry Island Unity Council amphitheater who was not shocked, scandalized — even traumatized — by the truth. A truth no one had even considered. For the first time, even the trio of Exalted Elders sat speechless.

The silence was broken by Fredo's sons, Tsuris and

Vey, who came charging down the center of the amphitheater, faces scarlet with rage. "It's a trick!" Tsuris yelled. "She did something, she made you all blind! My father is innocent!"

"Tell them, Uncle Thantos," Vey pleaded, reaching out to the mighty tracker. Thantos roughly shook the boy away. Without a word, he got up, turning to stalk out of the amphitheater.

His move jolted Ileana out of her shock. "No! I command you to stay!" she shouted. "I don't know what you did to her, to Leila, but you made her lie! You would revile the spirit of your own mother, anything to save your murderous skin!"

Thantos spun toward her. He opened his mouth to say something, then closed it abruptly. Staring at Ileana, he seemed to lose certainty. With a strange, almost pitiful glance at Karsh, the hulking tracker fell back into his chair and stared glumly at the trio of Exalted Elders.

"Let our father have his say!" Tsuris demanded. "He will clear this up!"

"He fears nothing! We fear nothing!" Vey called.

"Quiet!" Lady Rhianna, angry, shaken, but dignified as ever, found her voice and turned back to her old friend. "Karsh, what say you?"

Karsh's eyes filled with tears. He'd known — a part of him, anyway — that it hadn't been Thantos. But he never suspected it was Fredo. That the youngest son's stupidity was more dangerous than Thantos's power. He nodded at Rhianna. "Let him speak."

Fredo was overjoyed. The manic, goat-bearded warlock gloated. "Like Mama said, I'm the one, the man, the warlock! I flattened Aron with a stone. With one single heavy-duty rock. You wouldn't believe how much damage one rock can do. I didn't even believe it. But I had to make a choice. Aron even asked me to. He said, 'Whose side are you on, Fredo?' So I showed him."

"I don't believe you!" Ileana shouted.

"Why not?" Fredo asked innocently. "I didn't mean to take Aron out of the game for good. I just wanted to show my other brother — you know, Thantos — how solid I was for him. They used to argue all the time. I mean, I thought Thantos would be ecstatic. But, oh, boy, was he ever mad at me."

"You're lying," Ileana accused. "Why are you lying for him?"

"How can you accuse me of lying, fair Ileana? It was you who summoned up a witness. You who called on the spirit of the dead to appear here. You wanted the truth, you got it."

Thantos hauled himself to his feet. "Haven't we had enough of this grim circus?" he thundered.

Stubbornly, Ileana refused to believe it. "Of course

you'd like to stop him now. Now that he's lied to clear your name!"

"Can I tell her?" Fredo's glittering snake eyes turned pleadingly to his brother. "Oh, please, let me tell her."

"No!" Karsh called. "Lord Thantos is right. Enough is enough."

"But Karsh," Ileana protested. "Something must have happened. I must have done the spell wrong. Or . . ." She narrowed her fierce eyes at Thantos. "He tampered with her spirit!! He's powerful and mean enough to do it. He made her say it was Fredo!"

Even as she shouted it, Leila's words echoed in her ears, *Be careful what you wish for . . .*

Shaking her head, to rid herself of the terrible truth she must have known, but denied, Ileana shouted, "Fredo is just saying all that to get Thantos off the hook. Obviously, Fredo's going back to prison. By confessing to Aron's death, he spares the evil tracker, his murdering brother, the pain and shame due him. We can't let the monster get away with —"

"Monster? Evil tracker?" Fredo flashed his swamp eyes at her greedily. "He is your father, Ileana."

"No," she railed. "Liar! You're crazy, Fredo!"

"Mad as Miranda," he agreed. "But is that any way to talk to your uncle?"

Thantos rose and stalked from the chamber, his

hands coiled into fists, his hobnail boots echoing menac-
ingly.

"Uncle T, yo, wait," his nephew Vey hollered.

"You can't leave our father," Tsuris raged. "Not after
all he's done for you. He only killed Aron because he
knew you wanted him to. And what about us?"

"Yeah." Vey smirked. "We polished off that chump
photographer for you, didn't we?"

Ileana covered her ears and stood shaking in
Karsh's arms. The old warlock held her gently as she
buried her face in his warm velvet waistcoat. "It can't be
true," she sobbed. "Karsh, dear guardian, my oldest
friend, tell me that he is lying."

But even as she urged the faithful warlock to say
otherwise, Ileana knew that Fredo had told her the truth.
Lord Thantos, the greedy tracker she despised, the twins'
evil uncle against whom she'd fought to protect them
since the day of their birth, was her father.

CHAPTER TWENTY-ONE
SAYING HELLO

Cam connected with Brianna nearly every day — whenever Alex wasn't on-line playing nuthouse Nancy Drew, or getting Cam to unscramble some cyber-mess she'd clicked herself into.

At first, Bree's replies, some short, others long rants, upset Cam. Brianna was sullen, angry at "being here," at being forced to eat, gaining a "flabalanche" of weight! She wasn't sure where "here" was, and didn't care. Just that it was called Rolling Hills.

Her mom, on leave from her jobs, was staying in a nearby hotel and came to see her every day. Choosing between pride and her daughter's well-being, Mrs. Waxman finally accepted her ex-husband's offer of support. As for the Hollywood producer, he visited, too.

I had to get to this sick for him to pay attention to me, Bree wrote forlornly. How twisted is that?

But, after several weeks, Bree's e-mails steadily became more upbeat. Aside from her own therapy, she confided, the Waxmans were getting family counseling. It wasn't as if they'd gone from dys to functional in five easy sessions, but she'd actually gotten good and mad at her father and really let loose on him about his broken promises and messed-up priorities.

Of course, she'd broken down crying a minute later, but her shrink was totally proud of her. Brianna claimed the doc's Saturn would soon be wearing a bumper sticker that read: MY PATIENT IS AN HONOR NUT AT ROLLING HILLS.

Cam wished Alex was progressing as well. Her sister, the cyber-klutz, had gotten lost on a virtual tour of three facilities in San Diego. She'd printed out reams of clinic names and locations. Started receiving a ton of brochures from spas and sanitariums all over California. She compared the pictures in the flyers to the front-page photo in *Starstruck,* hoping to see just the right palm tree in front of just the right front entrance to make a match. No luck so far. She haunted celebrity websites and began reading *People* magazine to find out which asylums burnouts of the rich and famous frequented. There were hundreds of places, thousands.

California, Alex suggested, during week three of her clinic search, should be renamed the rehab state.

It wasn't until Bree began ragging on the "other loonies in the bin" that Cam knew she was actually getting better. Rolling Hills, Brianna explained, was like this huge buffet of sickos. The place was filled with substance abusers, eating disorder victims, depressives, bipolars, old-fashioned nervous breakdown sufferers, and rage-aholics in search of anger management techniques.

The ultimate bummer? She wasn't allowed to talk or write about who was actually there, or for what. "Even though every tabloid in the nation knows and tells," she grumbled. Much as it killed her not to dish, she confessed, she had decided to play by the rules.

Of course, the place was not perk-devoid, Bree eventually admitted. It was the ultimate in luxury. Great private rooms with plush carpeting, TVs, VCR, DVD and CD players, plus a media room, a spa, and a greenhouse-like solarium. Best of all was the pampering. "You get waited on hand and foot, you could live here," she joked. Though she wasn't planning to, there were others who were "lifers." There was even an on-site beauty salon, not that everyone used it. This one woman she'd gotten friendly with had not cut her hair since arriving — fifteen years ago!

"Fifteen years? What's the name of her place again?" Alex asked, getting out her list of clinic names.

"Rolling Hills. Why?" Cam wanted to know, although she'd gotten the same electric buzz at the number. "You're not thinking —"

"No, dude. No way." Alex's finger flew down the pages. Frustrated, she tossed the sheaf onto her bed. "Must be totally exclusive. It's not even listed!"

What about the guys? Beth had prodded Cam to ask.

Oh, yeah, it's a regular Hotties Anonymous, Bree reported drolly. Actually, she was surprisingly uninterested in boys. Call me crazy, she wrote — making Cam laugh — but the psycho-babes on campus are so not my thing. Mostly she hung with the woman with the long hair. "Rapunzel," Bree called her, like the fairy-tale princess.

There was something very regal about her. Which was weird, Bree knew, since in addition to blowing off the beauty salon, the woman didn't wear stitch one of makeup and never went anywhere without clutching this raggedy old quilt. She carried it to meals, the solarium, probably to the bath.

Alex was standing behind Cam, reading Bree's e-mail.

"A quilt?" Cam looked over her shoulder at her sister. "Didn't Karsh tell us once that Miranda had made us a patchwork quilt?"

Alex shrugged, but only because her lips had gone dry. And her heart was totally thudding.

The thing was, being with Quilt Woman made Bree feel good. Not like all happy and woo-hah, but . . . quietly good. Healthy. Oh, and don't tell Amanda, 'cause she'll like storm the place, but Rapunzel is way into herbs, candles, and crystals.

"Cam?" Alex said, her voice breaking. "It can't be, could it?" But before Cam got a chance to answer, Alex shook her head. "No way. Someone's messing with us."

"Either that or —"

"Or what?!" Alex challenged, balking suddenly at the possibility. She'd been pushing Cam, telling her they had to find their mother. But was she herself really ready? Now? Ready to be disappointed?

She's got this New Agey vibe going, Brianna reported in another e-mail. She'll be staring into space, sitting there wrapped in her old quilt, but the minute I show up — me or this other kid I'm bonding with, a well-known teen actress whose identity must remain a secret except to say she got busted for shoplifting and it was all over the news two weeks ago . . . When either of us shows up, Rapunzel snaps out of her trance and turns into this full-out mama bear. Totally there. And she'll ask, I don't know, all the right questions, the kind that get you to really open up. She's an amazing listener. She seems to understand everything. There's something different about her.

Different. Hadn't that been what Cam and Alex had felt all their lives? Was "Rapunzel" different the way they were?

"It's her," Cam said one day, a minute before her cell phone rang. They both jumped. "I didn't mean the phone. I meant Bree's . . . friend. It's Miranda, Alex."

"We don't know that for sure," her sister cautioned.

Cam pressed TALK. Brianna was on the phone, sounding distressingly, in Alex's opinion, like her old manic monologue-ing self. Today's call was all about the shopping trips Bree was now allowed to take — in addition to the phone privileges she'd earned. "Not that there are many designer stores in the 'hood," Alex heard her complain to Cam.

The 'hood, they'd finally learned, was the small, privately owned island off the coast of California where Rolling Hills was located. Alex grabbed her guitar, with every intention of drowning out Brianna's latest tale.

"Oh, I've been meaning to tell you — Quilt Lady?" Bree reported. "She never dresses in anything but hospital robes, but I bought this top I thought would look so slammin' on her. When she tried it on the other day I noticed she's got this necklace. I never noticed it on her before, it's probably been hidden under her robe. But the necklace? If you put Alex's and your charms together, it would look sort of like hers."

Cam was afraid to speak.

Alex tossed her bass on the bed and quickly filched the phone from her. "What's her name?" she asked. "Besides 'Rapunzel'?"

"Minda. Minda something. I don't know," Brianna said casually.

Cam found her voice and the twins began cautiously to lob questions at Bree. They found out the woman was "a lifer." That Bree wasn't sure why she was there, but she did seem kinda moony and depressed a lot. "Her story is a weeper," Brianna conceded. "Her husband was killed — and she only has this one strange-o visitor. Scary guy. Massive and mean-looking. Black beard, boots that are so lumberjack."

My vision! Cam sent an excited telepathic message to Alex. *The one I had before? Of a woman with a long braid, staring out a big window? There were all these colors — like a patchwork quilt! Als, could it be an . . . ?*

Epic coincidence, or evil master plan? Alex fin-

ished the thought. *Thantos said he'd bring us to her.*
"Yo, Breeski," she said, "can you hold on a minute?"

"But is he powerful enough to have engineered
Brianna being at the same place he stashed our mother?"
Cam asked, as Alex clamped her hand over the receiver.
"Is this how he's finally going to lure us? Or are we being
galactically paranoid?"

Cam snatched back the phone. "Bree, is there a very,
very sunny room at Rolling Hills, one filled with plants?"

"Hello. Did I mention our sunroom? That's like
Rapunzel headquarters." The phone flew back and forth
as they plied Bree with questions. The woman was sort
of average height, had auburn hair, they learned. "She's
the one who never cut it, wears it in a braid down her
back," Brianna reminded them. "Gray eyes, sometimes
they look kind of dull, but other times, they do resemble
yours. Age: indeterminate." And now that she thought
about it, the woman seemed to seek out Bree.

"She asks me about where I live, what I think about
things. She's really easy to talk to. And you know what's
really funny? Funny weird, not funny ha-ha. Of all the
doctors and shrinks in this place? Minda's the one I can
talk to about the really deep stuff. We talk about my dad,
how he's acted like a jerk. Like how one day maybe, if I'm
lucky, I'll be okay being me. At whatever weight." Bree
added thoughtfully, "She hardly talks to anyone else. Just

me and Jocelyn — oops, I mean, my anonymous famous shoplifting friend."

"Did she ever talk about . . . I mean, does she have kids?" Cam's voice cracked.

"Lost. Lost babies she once said. Who'd be about my age," Bree answered.

"More than one? Two lost babies?"

Later that night, they sat together in their room, staring at the phone. "It's not like I had a vision today," Cam reminded Alex.

"I know. I didn't catch a scent or hear a standby," Alex said.

"But she's going to call, right?"

"Soon," Alex decided. "Are your hands clammy?"

"No. My neck." Cam tugged at the collar of her sweater. "I'm hot and cold and sweating."

When the phone in their bedroom rang, she and Alex just stared at it. They knew who was calling.

A second ago, a buzzing had started in Alex's ears. "Oh, no. What if I can't hear her?"

As if she were getting a premonition, Cam's eyes started to sting.

"Aren't you going to answer it?" Alex rasped.

Slowly, Cam reached for the receiver. Alex's hand whipped past and pressed speakerphone.

A soft, whispery voice asked, "May I speak to . . . Apolla? I'm sorry, I mean, Camryn? Camryn Barnes?"

Cam's body turned to jelly. "This is," Cam managed to squeak.

Alex was hyperventilating. There was silence on the other end. "And . . . Artem — Is Alexandra also there?"

"Yes," Alex practically shouted, then lowering her voice she said, "This is Artemis. Apolla is here, too. . . ."

They could hear crying on the other end of the phone. Suddenly, Cam's face was wet. When she spoke again her voice was thick with tears. "Is it really you?" she sobbed.

"Are you all right?" Alex asked, trembling.

Suddenly, it didn't matter if Thantos had masterminded the whole thing. It didn't matter if he had used Brianna, or was now using Miranda, their mother, to lure them — or if he intended to put their powers to work for him.

The person they'd been searching for ever since they'd met was close enough to — "Can we come to you?" Cam sputtered.

"Soon," Miranda responded, clearing her throat. "Very soon. I'll come to you."

"Can you leave Rolling Hills? Will they let you leave? How will you get here?" Alex blurted.

"I can. There's just been no reason before. I

haven't — not in fifteen years. But if you are my babies, my lost babies —" Miranda couldn't continue.

Why didn't you come for us? Alex only thought it, but through the phone, from 3,000 miles away, her mother heard. And answered.

"I was sick. And when I began to get well, I asked for you. And I was told you had not survived."

"He told you that? Thantos?" Alex asked bitterly.

"And you believed it?" Cam wanted to know.

"In my heart, I never gave up hope. Apolla. Artemis. My lost babies." Miranda could barely speak. "I'll see you —"

"Wait!" Cam said, terrified that their mother would hang up, and somehow be lost to them again, this time forever. "Don't go! I mean, where — are you coming here, to the house? When? Where can we meet you? Where will you be?"

"At the tree," Miranda said. "I've pictured you there so many times. A gnarled old oak tree on a hill in a park overlooking a harbor. Is there such a place?"

"Mariner's Park," Cam said.

"But when?" Alex asked.

"Soon," Miranda promised.

ABOUT THE AUTHORS

H.B. Gilmour is the author of numerous best-selling books for adults and young readers, including the *Clueless* movie novelization and series; *Pretty in Pink,* a University of Iowa Best Book for Young Readers; and *Godzilla,* a Nickelodeon Kids Choice nominee. She also cowrote the award-winning screenplay *Tag.*

H.B. lives in upstate New York with her husband, John Johann, and their misunderstood dog, Fred, one of the family's five pit bulls, three cats, two snakes (a boa constrictor and a python), and five extremely bright, animal-loving children.

Randi Reisfeld has written many best-sellers, such as the *Clueless* series (which she wrote with H.B.); the *Moesha* series; and biographies of Prince William, New Kids on the Block, and Hanson. Her Scholastic paperback *Got Issues Much?* was named an ALA Best Book for Reluctant Readers in 1999.

Randi has always been fascinated with the randomness of life . . . About how any of our lives can simply "turn on a dime" and instantly (*snap!*) be forever changed. About the power each one of us has deep inside, if only we knew how to access it. About how any of us would react if, out of the blue, we came face-to-face with our exact double.

From those random fascinations, T*Witches was born.

Oh, and BTW: She has no twin (that she knows of) but an extremely cool family and cadre of BFFs to whom she is totally devoted.